RAIN OF FIRE

Also by Marion Dane Bauer

Shelter from the Wind

Foster Child

Tangled Butterfly

RAIN OF FIRE

Marion Dane Bauer

CLARION BOOKS

TICKNOR & FIELDS:
A HOUGHTON MIFFLIN COMPANY

NEW YORK

Clarion Books
Ticknor & Fields, a Houghton Mifflin Company

Printed in the U.S.A.

Library of Congress Cataloging in Publication Data

Bauer, Marion Dane.
Rain of fire.

Summary: When Steve's older brother Matthew, returning home after service in World War II, refuses to talk about his wartime experiences, Steve's friends begin to doubt the stories he has told of Matthew's heroism.
1. World War, 1939–1945 – Juvenile fiction.
[1. World War, 1939–1945 – Fiction. 2. War – Fiction.
3. Heroes – Fiction] I. Title.
PZ7.B3262Rai 1983 [Fic] 83-2065
ISBN 0-89919-190-8

V 10 9 8 7 6 5 4

For my mother,
Elsie Hempstead Dane,
and my Japanese daughter,
Mami Hirano, with love

CHAPTER 1

"What's a foxhole good for if you've got only one?" Celestino asked. "You can't have a war all in the same foxhole."

Steve stood on the edge of the hole, three feet deep and six feet square, that he and the twins had spent most of the summer digging, and sized up Celestino. Celestino was new in the neighborhood. He was fourteen, two years older and a full head taller than Steve and the twins. And he criticized the foxhole without even bothering to walk over to see it properly. Instead he leaned against an oak tree on the edge of the clearing and cleaned his fingernails with the blade of a jackknife.

"We've only just finished this one," Kenny said, always the first of the twins to speak.

"What'd you expect anyway?" Steve asked.

"Me?" Celestino shrugged, the muscles below his rolled T-shirt sleeves rippling slightly. "I didn't expect nothin'. You're the ones wanted to bring me out to the middle of this forest to show me your secret hideout."

"It's not a forest," Donny explained. "It's only a woods."

A woodpecker made its machine-gun *rat-a-tat-tat* deep inside the green gloom of the trees.

Celestino snapped the jackknife closed and slipped it into the pocket of his blue jeans. "It don't matter to me what you call it," he said. "There's still nothing you can do with just one foxhole."

"We're going to dig another," Steve said. "We planned to all along, but it takes time." He glanced sideways at the twins to see if either one would say anything. The three of them *hadn't* talked about digging another foxhole; they had been glad to be done with this one. The twins didn't usually contradict anything Steve said, though, and they didn't this time either.

"If I had me a couple of sticks of dynamite," Celestino said, stepping closer to the three boys, "I could fix you guys up with another foxhole quick enough." Celestino's dark eyes gleamed. He struck an imaginary match and held it to an invisible fuse in the air in front of him.

Steve watched, fascinated, as Celestino's hands described the shape and size of the dynamite, the rapidly diminishing fuse.

"Boom!" Celestino exploded, his hands flying apart, and Steve jerked involuntarily. When Celestino smiled at him, his white teeth gleaming, Steve knew that he had given the older boy exactly the reaction he wanted.

"Huh," Steve said, stuffing his fists into his pockets – it hadn't been his idea to invite this new kid to their hideout – "what do you know about dynamite?"

Celestino pushed his chin out. "My old man blew up Jap

bridges in the war. Bridges and roads. You name it, and my old man blew it up."

Steve scoffed. "If that's true, how come he's night watchman in the quarry? They'd have him setting charges if he knew about dynamite and stuff like that."

"Because his dad got wounded, Steve," Kenny jumped in to explain. "You saw the way he walks with one leg stiff."

"Yeah," Donny added. "He wouldn't be able to get away fast enough after he lit the fuse. Not with that bum leg."

Celestino nodded his agreement sharply.

Steve changed the subject, though he still didn't believe Celestino's story. "My brother was in the army, too. Matthew was artillery."

"Did he get a Purple Heart?" Celestino asked, stepping closer so that he towered over Steve, making Steve feel short . . . and even fat, though he wasn't really fat. He tugged on the front of his shirt and tried to draw in his belly.

"My old man got a Purple Heart," Celestino said. The statement was a challenge.

"Matthew was never wounded," Kenny explained, filling in for Steve's silence.

"He just got home a couple of months ago," Donny added.

Celestino looked dubious. "What was he doing for so long? The war's been over for a whole year."

"He was in the army of occupation," Kenny continued.

Donny nodded. "In Japan."

"Yeah," Steve said, wishing the twins would quit speaking for him, "and he has a medal . . . more important than a Purple Heart. It's for 'bravery above and beyond the call of duty.'"

Kenny gasped. "He does?"

"You never told us that before." Donny's words were sharp with accusation.

"Well, he does."

"My old man's got a bayonet he took off a dead Jap," Celestino offered.

"Anybody can take stuff off a dead man," Steve said. "You have to *earn* a medal."

Celestino narrowed his eyes. "What'd your brother do to earn a medal if he didn't get wounded?"

Steve brushed at some gnats that hovered in front of his face. "The medal was for bravery, I told you." And then he added pointedly, "You don't have to be brave to get wounded, you know. You only have to be in the way."

Celestino ran the tip of his tongue over his lips. "That depends on what you was doing when you got wounded. If it happened when you was blowing up an important bridge . . . while the Japs were trying to cross it . . ." He let the sentence hang in midair.

This guy's really good, Steve thought grudgingly. *He can tell a fib without ever saying it all the way.* "You'd have to be pretty dumb to blow yourself up with it," he said, his voice held calm and cool to match Celestino's.

"Shrapnel," Celestino supplied, brushing away his own gnats. "All the way to the bone. They couldn't get it out. What did your brother do?"

Steve hiked up his blue jeans, pulled down the front of his shirt again. "He rescued a whole bunch of his buddies. They were surrounded by Japs, and he rescued them all."

The twins were staring, first at Steve, then at Celestino.

They might have been watching a Ping-Pong match. Steve kept his eyes on Celestino's face and on the dark, arched eyebrow that rose a fraction of an inch.

"And how'd he do that?" Celestino inquired.

Steve sighed, pretending to be bored with the subject, pretending that he had told the story so many times he hated to have to go through it again. "Well, he was on the howitzer . . . see?"

Celestino nodded abruptly.

"And all of a sudden he realized the Japs were trying to surround them. They were already in front of him and on two sides."

"So he turned the howitzer on them," Celestino concluded, tapping down a yawn with one hand.

"It's obvious," Steve said, glancing up at Celestino scornfully, "that you don't know much about howitzers. These Japs were too close for the big gun."

"So what did he do?" Kenny demanded, breathless, his blue-violet eyes wide and his dark hair standing in exclamation points all over his head.

"The only thing he *could* do," Steve replied. "He led his men out."

Donny put both hands up to secure his sailor hat. He was wearing no shirt – the twins always went shirtless in the summer and turned as brown as nuts – and his ribs stood out like the ridges on a washboard. "Didn't the Japs shoot at them . . . at Matthew and his buddies?"

"Of course they did," Steve answered, standing up straighter. "They tried to kill Matthew and all his buddies, but my brother outfoxed them."

"How?" Kenny was leaning forward to catch every word. "What'd he do?"

Steve leaned toward them confidingly. "Matthew had these grenades, see? And he threw them. Every minute or so he'd pull a pin and throw another grenade . . . right out in front of where he could see the muzzles of their guns. The noise and the smoke were so bad they nearly drove the Japs crazy."

Steve paused, checked out his audience. The twins were listening intently, as they always did when Steve was telling something good. Celestino was examining his fingernails again. *He must have the dirtiest nails in town*, Steve thought, but he continued. "The Japs couldn't see to hit anybody. Every single guy got out alive, and Matthew went out last of all. Only after he had thrown his last grenade."

"How many Japs did he kill?" Kenny asked. "It must have been a whole bunch."

Steve straightened up and sucked in his breath. "I didn't say Matthew killed anybody. I told you he threw the grenades out in front of the Japs. They made a smoke screen that way. What Matthew did was a lot more dangerous than killing people, because they could still shoot, see?"

"But why – " Donny was starting to ask when Celestino interrupted.

"Gunners don't have no grenades," Celestino said.

"Huh?" Steve turned slowly from the twins to face Celestino.

"I said," Celestino repeated, "they don't give gunners no grenades."

Steve could feel his face going hot. What right did this kid have, interfering in his story? He hadn't said a thing about

Celestino's father going around blowing up Jap bridges, getting filled with shrapnel. "Well, maybe," he said, his words stumbling, "maybe he wasn't on the big gun that day. Maybe I just forgot."

"And maybe you made the whole thing up," Celestino said. "Like you did about the medal. Unless your big brother got a medal from the medics for being funny in the head."

One of the twins giggled. Steve didn't see which one it was. He glowered fiercely in their direction and then turned his scowl on Celestino. "What are you talking about?"

"You know what I'm talking about, Pulaski." Celestino emphasized the *ass* in the middle of Pulaski. "I seen your big brother. He's the guy mopes around all the time like a sick cow. He don't have a job or nothing."

"Well, he's going to get a job," Steve protested. "Any day he's going to get one. Or maybe he'll go back to college. He was in college when he got drafted, you know."

"That so?" Obviously Celestino wasn't impressed.

"And he does have a medal. Only he won't show it to anybody. He keeps it locked away all the time."

"How'd you come to see it, then?" Celestino was looking toward the twins, including them in his idea of a joke.

"He showed it to me because – "

"Because you're nobody. Right?"

"Because I'm his brother, dummy. What do you think?"

"I don't think. I know."

"What is it you think you know?"

"That you're a liar." Celestino stepped in close so that Steve had to crane his neck to meet the taller boy's gaze. They stood that way for a moment, confronting one another.

Steve gave no ground, even though he was feeling shorter and pudgier with each passing second. A smile flitted across Celestino's face and he added softly, "Blubber-butt."

Steve stepped back as if he had been slapped, and he looked toward Kenny and Donny to come to his defense. Nobody had ever called him such a name before, not in all his life, and in front of his best friends! But there stood Kenny, his face split by a wide grin, and though Donny was watching intently, he wasn't saying a word.

"Blubber-butt," Kenny repeated to himself, like someone trying out a name for fit, and then he began to laugh. Celestino joined him, his laugh squeezed out in a long string, and finally Donny started, too, doubling over and slapping one knee.

"Blubber-butt," they all repeated together, and Steve turned and walked stiffly across the clearing, holding his breath, holding his stomach in, holding himself from exploding into a thousand pieces.

CHAPTER 2

Steve thrashed through the underbrush blindly. He didn't even watch for itch weed or poison ivy, and he was usually careful about that. If he got poison ivy, he didn't get a little rash; he swelled up until his face looked like a tomato – as red and as smooth and shiny. But right now he didn't care. He wouldn't have cared if he'd walked through a nest of snakes.

He kicked at a dead limb lying in his path and cursed when he hurt his foot.

Where did the twins come off laughing like that? This new kid showed up, and just because he was bigger, just because he was older, they fell in with him. The twins had no loyalty to anyone but each other. They never had. It was as if, having the other twin always there, they didn't need to worry about keeping friends.

So what if Celestino came from Chicago. That didn't make him anything special. In fact, it made him pretty dumb – calling a woods in the middle of Illinois a forest. Calling Matthew funny in the head, just because he didn't have a job yet. Calling Steve Blubber-butt.

And the twins had laughed. Now the name would probably follow him to school when it started up again. He would be called Blubber-butt for the rest of his life.

Not fat, his mother always said, *only chubby. The same as Matthew was when he was your age*. But it was hard to imagine Matthew's ever being fat – or chubby either, for that matter. Steve had been pretty little when Matthew was twelve, though. Maybe he didn't remember what Matthew looked like then.

What difference did it make anyway? Nobody had ever called Matthew Blubber-butt. Steve was sure of that.

He emerged from the woods to an alfalfa field and the sharp sunshine of the August afternoon. The alfalfa field and then a corn field separated the woods from the highway and the dust-colored cement mill from the double row of houses reserved for the families of men who worked at the mill. The wood-frame houses faced one another across a red-slag street, the slag left over from years before when this had been a coal-mining town instead of a cement-milling one.

"I'll get that Celestino," Steve said to the grasshoppers whirring ahead of his feet. "You just wait and see if I don't."

Celestino had no right challenging other people's stories like that. So maybe gunners weren't issued grenades. How was Steve supposed to know things like that when Matthew wouldn't tell him the least little thing about any of it? Before Matthew had gone off to war, he'd always been telling Steve things, stories about elves who had defended themselves against a marauding crow and knights who did battle with terrible dragons. All little kid stuff, but still it had been fun.

Now, when Matthew had real stories to tell – must have,

you couldn't be in a war and not have lots of exciting stories – he wouldn't tell Steve a thing. It wasn't anything gory Steve wanted to hear, like stories about killing people. Steve knew Matthew hadn't killed anybody, whatever the twins said. He was on a big gun, and the big gun shot at targets, not people.

The alfalfa Steve crushed beneath each step perfumed the air with its fresh sweetness. The puffy white column of smoke from the mill stack rolled against a brilliant blue sky. And Steve could feel the rage already seeping away, as though it trickled out the ends of his fingers and toes. That was one of his problems. He could never stay mad at anybody long enough to do any good. His friends all knew it, too.

He would stay mad at Celestino, though.

He stepped out of the alfalfa onto the street. Several houses down, on the sidewalk in front of Steve's house, Rebecca Hansen was bouncing a golf ball, obviously waiting for Steve to show up. Steve started walking faster. He would show the twins that he didn't need to wait around for them to feel like playing. Besides, Becca could probably help him figure out some way to get even with Celestino. She was good at ideas. Almost as good as Steve was at stories.

When he came up behind Becca, he could hear her chanting as she bounced the ball, "My name is Teresa and my husband's name is Tim, and I come from Toledo with a carload of toads." Her taffy-blond ponytail swung with the rhythm of the ball, and when she said each *T* word, she lifted one leg, circling the ball. It was an alphabet game that had been popular with all the girls in the sixth grade during the last weeks of school. Steve thought it was dumb.

"My name is Ursula," she continued, ignoring Steve or not

aware of him, "and my husband's name is Unk, and we come from Utah with a carload of – "

"Unk! What sort of a name is Unk?" Steve passed Becca and flopped down on his front steps.

Becca caught the ball, pocketed it, and looked at Steve as if he were impossibly dumb, which was her favorite way to look at people. It was the reason she and the twins didn't play together much. Becca and Kenny usually fought.

"Nobody in all this world has ever been named Unk," Steve persisted.

"That's what you think. We call my uncle Bob Unk all the time."

"But that's just short for *uncle*. It's not a name."

"It's as good as one." Becca put her hand in the other pocket of her shorts and came up with a Salerno butter cookie on one finger like a scalloped ring. Amazingly, it wasn't broken. She began nibbling the scallops off the edge of the cookie.

Steve looked away from the cookie and asked, "What were they going to have a carload of?"

"Who?"

"Ursula and Unk. What were they bringing from Utah?"

"Ukeleles," she answered, turning the cookie and biting away each bump on the edge.

She would keep at it that way until she had only the scallop that represented the diamond of the ring left on the top. Steve had seen her do it before. If he had the cookie, he would eat it in two bites. "What do you use for *X*?"

"I skip *X*. Nothing begins with *X* except for X-ray and xylophone."

"What about *Z*?"

"Zelda and Zeke. They come from the Zephyr with a carload of zebras."

"Hah!" Steve cried, triumphant. He had her there. "The Zephyr isn't a place you can come from, it's the name of a train. A streamliner."

"I know," Becca replied. "And Zelda and Zeke like to ride the Zephyr."

Steve slapped his forehead and stood up to go in. There was no reasoning with some people.

"Anyway," Becca said, holding her hand out to examine her cookie ring, "what makes you so crabby?"

Steve sat down again. He didn't know why he hadn't simply told Becca first thing. She always heard what people didn't say louder than what they were talking about. "There's this new kid just moved in – "

"Ray Celestino," she supplied. She took another critical look at her diamond, wriggled the cookie carefully off her finger, and handed it to Steve.

Steve nodded gratefully. "Yeah, that's his name. Celestino. Well, he's a real bully. He's already taken over my foxhole . . . and the twins." He popped the remainder of the cookie into his mouth.

"And they let him?" Becca asked, her slightly tilted, cat-green eyes blinking with surprise. Nobody, but *nobody* would ever take over Becca.

"Oh, they thought he was a real funny man." Steve wasn't going to tell Becca about the name Celestino had used that the twins thought was so amusing. He didn't think Becca would laugh, but you could never tell. He hadn't expected the twins to laugh either.

"What are you going to do?" Becca asked.

Steve propped his chin in his hands so that his entire head bumped up and down when he chewed. "What's there to do?" he asked mournfully. "The twins follow him around like puppies."

"Maybe you could figure out some way to get rid of him," Becca suggested. "Like getting his family to move back to Chicago."

Steve thought about that. The only people who could live in the mill housing were the men who worked at the mill and their families. "Maybe I should tell your father that Celestino's old man ought to be fired. He wasn't even a good soldier. He blew up his own leg." Becca's father was the superintendent of the entire mill and could fire anyone he wanted to.

The screen door squeaked open behind them and then tapped closed again. "Who wasn't a good soldier?" Matthew asked, stopping in the middle of the porch.

"Nobody," Steve answered, glancing back at his brother. But then it occurred to Steve that Matthew might think they had been talking about him, so he explained, "Mr. Celestino. Ray Celestino's father."

"Why are you worrying about what kind of a soldier he was?" Matthew asked, a little curtly. "The war is over – or didn't you kids hear?"

Steve could feel himself flushing. Matthew had never talked to him like that before he had gone off to the army. They used to be friends, even if there were nine years between them. "His son cares, for one," Steve said. "He was bragging on his dad, saying he used to blow up Jap bridges."

"Maybe he did," Matthew answered, but his voice sounded

a little vague, and he was gazing down the street toward the woods.

"He was talking about you, too. He said you were—" Steve stopped. He couldn't say the rest, even if Matthew did make him mad.

Steve felt Matthew's hand on the top of his head, a gentle, firm pressure. "Don't listen to things people say, Steve. People saying it doesn't make it true."

For a moment Steve sat where he was, enjoying the familiar, reassuring presence, but then he ducked his head forward, dislodging Matthew's hand, and asked, "Were you really fat . . . chubby when you were my age, like Mom says?"

Matthew came down the steps between Becca and Steve, turned around, and studied Steve's face. "Has somebody been giving you a hard time?"

Steve poked at a hole in the toe of his black, high-topped tennis shoe, tried to look nonchalant. "He tried. That's all. He doesn't really bother me, though."

"Who's *he*?"

"Celestino."

"He took over the twins and the foxhole, too," Becca filled in.

At the word *foxhole*, Matthew's face slammed shut. "I don't understand what you need a foxhole for anyway . . . or why you would want to play war."

"You used to play war when you were a kid, didn't you?" Becca asked.

"No," he replied sharply. "I never did."

"You and me used to play knights in the forest primeval all the time," Steve objected.

"You and I," Matthew corrected automatically, but he didn't look at Steve.

"You and I," Steve repeated, "before you went into the army. You had wooden swords and everything . . . painted silver. What ever happened to those things?"

Matthew turned and started up the walk without answering.

"Do you know where they are?" Steve called after him.

Matthew turned back sharply. His square-jawed, friendly face was set in a deep scowl. The sun glinted off his coppery hair, kept cropped short to discourage the red-gold curls both Matthew and Steve shared with their mother. "It was a stupid game," he said, "and I don't know where the swords are. And I think you would do well to stay away from Ray Celestino."

"Why?" Steve asked, defiance rising, as if he *wanted* to get near Celestino. "What's wrong with him?"

Matthew shrugged, a small, tight movement of the muscles that strained the shoulders of his faded blue shirt. "Nothing, maybe, but I've met his father, and he's a bad sort. You'd do best to stay clear of the whole family."

"I don't think there's anything wrong with Mr. Celestino," Steve replied. He could feel the weight of his own sullen lower lip, but he didn't know why he was arguing. Steve had no interest in Ray Celestino's father. But then he added casually, "He has a bayonet that he took off a dead Jap."

Matthew's face changed shape, curiously, several times, his jaw working like the jaw of some old man about to let loose with a stream of tobacco juice. Steve waited for what his brother would say, but Matthew didn't say anything at all. He simply turned on his heel and, without glancing back, strode to the end of the sidewalk and down the road in the direction of the woods.

"Maybe he's going to tell Celestino a thing or two," Steve muttered, but he knew that wasn't what Matthew was going to do. He was just running off to walk in the woods. That was practically all he had done since he'd come home from the army, walk in the woods and smoke. "I've got to think some things through," Matthew would say. "What he needs is a job to go to," was their father's opinion. But their mother always said, "Give him time. He just needs time," and their father would snort to show what he thought of Matthew's needing time.

"Matthew gets awfully mad when anybody talks about the war, doesn't he?" Becca asked, a studied innocence in her voice.

Steve stood up abruptly and started around the walk to the back of the house. He wished Becca would go home. He wished Celestino had stayed in Chicago where he belonged.

He even wished they were all still waiting for Matthew to come back from the war.

CHAPTER 3

Steve sat down on the slanting cellar doors next to the back steps. He glanced from the sodden, still sheets on the clothesline to the hens scratching inside their small pen on one side of the yard. A vegetable garden took up most of the end of the yard, and he thought of picking a tomato and getting some salt from the kitchen to eat it with. Matthew used to make him tomato sandwiches, just two slices of bread and thick, juicy slices of tomato from their mother's garden.

It had seemed forever, the three years they had waited for Matthew to come home. Their family had done everything they could to help the war effort, saved all their cans and other bits of metal to be taken away to factories and made into tanks and bombs. They had patched sheets and conserved gas and gone without meat. Steve's mother had even taken to drawing a line on the back of her legs to look like the seam of silk stockings so she didn't have to buy stockings.

They had called the garden a Victory Garden, too. That's what President Roosevelt had called them when he was still alive, though Steve had never understood how spinach and radishes could help win a war.

When the radio had announced that the U.S. had wiped out the whole city of Hiroshima with a single powerful bomb, that Japan was about to surrender and the war would be over at last, Steve's mother had gone into her garden and planted marigold seeds up and down the rows of vegetables. It had been practically the middle of August, much too late to be planting flowers, but she didn't care.

"They'll never bloom," Steve's father had said.

"At least they'll have a chance," Mother answered. "Now they can have a chance." And she went on planting.

The flowers had bloomed, rows and rows of gold and bronze, the small heads emerging through the dying vegetables. Steve had loved those marigolds. He'd brought practically the entire neighborhood to see the display. Everyone had seen them except Matthew. By the time he had come home, the garden was vegetables again.

Lots of things had changed by the time Matthew had come home . . . especially Matthew.

Steve could hear Becca coming around the corner of the house, bouncing her golf ball on the sidewalk as she moved. Each time the ball hit the walk, it made a sharp clicking sound. Somebody else might have figured she wasn't wanted and gone home, but not Becca.

"Do you want to hear something about Celestino?" he asked, turning to face her as she approached. "Something nobody else knows?"

"Sure." She caught the ball and came to a stop in front of the cellar doors where Steve sat.

"He steals bikes," Steve said, speaking the words with deliberate distinctness.

Becca frowned. "When he lived in Chicago, you mean? He couldn't get away with stealing bikes around here, unless he gets them in town."

Steve wiped his palms on the front of his shirt. "I don't know what he did in Chicago," he said, "because I wasn't there, but here he steals bikes, probably from town. He takes them up behind his garage and paints them so they're disguised."

Becca looked unconvinced. "Then what does he do with them?"

"Sells them. What do you think?" Steve lowered his voice. "He probably has connections with the Mafia in Chicago. Those guys wouldn't have any trouble unloading a few stolen bikes."

Becca turned the golf ball over in her hand, bounced it a couple of times, and peered at Steve as if checking to see if he was still there. "How do you know?" she asked.

Steve stood up, walked down the slanting door to the sidewalk next to Becca, and spoke in an urgent whisper. "I saw him. I was out a couple of nights ago – real late, I was looking for my mom's cat – and I saw him. He was up behind where all the garages are at the end of the street – behind the one where his dad keeps their car – painting this bike. It looked like a real expensive bike, too."

"How do you know it wasn't his?"

"Huh! Have you ever seen Celestino with an expensive bike? He rides that old junker without any fenders. Besides – " Steve bent closer to Becca's ear – "the one I saw couldn't have been Celestino's."

"Why not?" Becca seemed to be holding her breath, waiting to be convinced.

Steve rolled back on his heels, thrust his hands into his pockets, and spoke triumphantly, out loud now. "It was a girl's."

Becca studied Steve's face for a careful minute. "Steve Pulaski, are you telling the truth?"

Steve took another step back. "Cross my heart and hope to die!" He made a rapid crossing motion over his chest and raised his right hand in the air.

"Stick a needle in your eye?"

Steve nodded solemnly, though his other hand was behind his back with his fingers crossed. That was only a minor precaution, though. He wasn't really lying. Stealing bikes was the kind of thing someone like Celestino was sure to do.

Steve had only half-expected Becca to believe him – she wasn't as gullible as the twins – but gradually the skepticism on her face was replaced by a sly grin. "If only the twins knew Ray Celestino is a thief," she said, "that would fix him good."

"Yeah," Steve agreed. He squatted and pressed one finger on a red ant that had been scurrying along the sidewalk, then lifted the finger to his nose to smell the sharp, cinnamony scent the ant left behind. "But I don't suppose they would believe me even if I told them. They're on Celestino's side now."

"I know something the twins would believe." Becca's eyes were dancing the way they always did when she was coming up with one of her ideas.

"What?" Steve stood up. It was his turn to feel a little skeptical. Becca's ideas had a way of getting people into trouble – everybody except Becca. But still, there was a small balloon of excitement in his chest.

"If Celestino stole one of their bikes, stole it and painted it out behind his garage. If he did that and the twins found the bike there, they would believe he was a thief quick enough."

The balloon in Steve's chest deflated. "Celestino wouldn't be dumb enough to do that."

"Then," Becca said, shaking her ponytail until it swung wildly, "we'll have to steal one of their bikes for him."

Steve could feel his jaw going loose, feel his mouth hanging open. "Steal a bike? From Kenny or Donny? You've got to be kidding!" This was a wild idea even for Becca, and she was the one who, when they were smaller, had talked him into jumping out of the cottonwood tree in her backyard wearing a parachute she had made from a piece of sheet. Steve had sprained his ankle, and his father had said he was lucky the ankle hadn't been broken, considering how far he had fallen.

"Sure. But it won't really be stealing. They'll get it back. They'll get it back and be mad at Celestino for the rest of forever. What could be better?"

Steve tried to think. Surely there was something that would be better than stealing one of the twins' bikes and pretending Celestino had done it. "I don't know if that's such a good idea," he said slowly. "What if the twins' parents called the police? What if Celestino really got into trouble?"

"It would serve him right," Becca explained patiently. "It would make up for the times when he really stole kids' bikes and didn't get caught." But then Becca narrowed her eyes and took a step closer to Steve. "Unless you're making this whole thing up. Unless you never saw anything. Maybe Celestino doesn't steal bikes and paint them and sell them."

"Of course he does!" Steve exclaimed. "And I saw him, too." He glared at Becca until she couldn't outstare him any longer and she began examining a mosquito bite on her arm. "All I'm worried about," Steve explained then, "is the painting. They got those bikes new last Christmas."

"Oh, well." Becca shrugged. "If you don't think it's a good idea . . ."

"I didn't say that. I just need to think about it a minute. That's all."

Becca turned away and bounced her ball a few more times, while Steve tugged on his hair and pretended to think. Actually he wasn't thinking about anything at all. Words like *liar* and *Blubber-butt* chased one another through his brain.

"When the twins got their bikes," he said at last, "Donny felt real bad because Kenny got the red one."

"Yeah," Becca agreed, "and his was only blue."

"And I know where my dad has a can of red paint . . . on the shelf in the basement."

"And a brush?" Becca inquired.

"And a brush."

"When should we do it, then?"

Steve took a deep breath. "How about tonight? If you can get out after dark, you can meet me in the alley, just behind my chicken coop."

"Sure thing." Becca was grinning, but she clicked her sandals together and gave a smart salute. "Aye-aye, sir."

Steve groaned. "That's navy, Hansen. We're army around here." No wonder they didn't draft girls.

Becca shrugged and smiled more broadly. "I'll see you

tonight," she said, leaning forward and speaking in a loud stage whisper. "We'll carry out our secret mission in the face of every danger."

"Sure," Steve said. "In the face of every danger." He turned and started up the back steps. They would be doing Donny a favor, he reminded himself. Really. Donny always had wanted a red bike.

CHAPTER 4

"Where are you going so late at night?"

Steve stopped, frozen with one hand still on the screen door that he had closed stealthily behind him.

Matthew asked again. "Where are you going, little brother?"

"Out," Steve replied, releasing the handle of the door. "It's too hot to sleep."

Matthew sighed. "It sure is. You'd think it would cool off more when the sun goes down." He pushed out the door after Steve. "Not even a breath of wind. It feels like the armpit of hell," and then he added more softly, "like being back in that jungle."

Steve didn't say anything. He stood next to Matthew listening to the quiet rhythm of his breathing, waiting for him to go away. This was all Steve needed; just when he was ready to carry out his plan with Becca, his brother had decided to be pals. He wanted to talk about the war, even.

From inside the house, Steve could hear his parents' voices, the click of the big console radio in the living room being turned off, then the lights. He heard their footsteps on the stairs, heading up to their bedroom.

But Matthew wasn't going anywhere. He settled heavily on the step beside Steve, like a large watchdog devoted to his task. "Do you remember," he asked, his voice mellow, "when you were a real little guy, and I used to come in on hot summer nights and steal you out of your bed?"

"To swim in the stars and cool off. It's what you used to say. You even told me the stars were made of ice." Steve didn't mean for the words to be an accusation, but somehow they came out sounding that way.

Matthew sighed again, a great heaving of his back and shoulders. "Well, they're not, kid. I lied to you. They're not made of ice at all . . . only fire." Matthew sat hunched over in the darkness. "Nothing but fire," he added sadly.

Steve hated it when Matthew called him "kid." He never used to call Steve "kid" before, as though he'd forgotten his name. Nobody ever used to say Matthew was funny in the head either. They'd had no reason. "It's all right," Steve said now. "I never believed you anyway."

It was the wrong thing to say. Steve knew it was as soon as the words were out. Matthew stood up abruptly and turned back to the house. "Don't go far," was all he said as the screen door whooshed shut behind him.

Steve stood where he was, hugging his bare chest against a shiver that started someplace inside. A cricket was chirping from beneath the steps. Another answered from the grass. There didn't seem to be any way to be with Matthew these days without saying the wrong thing. There was something about the tight set of his jaw, the way his back curved, that made people – not just Steve – want to say angry things to him, or about him. It wasn't true, though, what Celestino had said. It was a worse lie than any story Steve made up.

Wearing only his blue jeans in the shielding darkness, Steve stepped onto the narrow strip of sidewalk that still held the heat from the day, and then onto the cooling grass. He walked slowly the length of the yard, savoring the coolness. The hens were all lined up on top of their coop, their heads tucked beneath their wings or accordion-pleated into their hunched forms, sleeping. Even the shadows and shapes of the vegetable garden seemed more still than they were during the day.

Steve stepped cautiously across the alley cinders and stopped on the edge of the corn field. The corn stood taller than his head, like an army of slender, many-armed soldiers. The faintly rustling stalks held darkness prisoner on the ground, away from the burning starlight and the thin white beams of a quarter moon. The day's heat was held there, too. Steve moved along the edge of the corn to the alfalfa field. There was a path through the alfalfa, created by the men who walked, morning, noon, and night, to and from the mill. This was where Becca would come, if she was able to get out. Her father's house, the mill superintendent's house, stood by itself on the other side of the field.

A light flashed on, stabbed along the ground, and settled into a bobbing movement that progressed toward Steve. Becca had brought a flashlight. Steve was glad she had thought of it. He hadn't been able to find his.

Steve moved a few steps along the path and stopped, waiting. Even from a distance, the probing, moving light made everything around it seem more black than it had been by moonlight.

Suddenly Steve wrapped his arms around his bare chest and shivered again, despite the heat. They were going to steal a bike. Not just any bike, but a bike that belonged to one of his best friends. Steve looked around, suddenly uneasy. The darkness of the woods, the inky heat that gathered at the base of the corn stalks, the shadows that fell behind the houses in response to the low, round-globed street lights all seemed vaguely threatening. He began to walk along the path, slowly at first, then faster, hurrying toward the swinging light.

"Becca," he called softly, "is that you?"

"It's me," she answered in a loud whisper. "Did you get the paint and a brush?"

"I got both. I put them out behind the chicken coop right after supper."

"Is that where we're going to do it? Behind your chicken coop?"

"I'm not working up by the garages, that's for sure. Somebody might see us."

"Good thinking. Now, where does Donny keep his bike?"

For a moment Steve almost wished that he didn't know. The missing link – no bike to steal. They'd both have to go home to bed. He could put the paint back in the basement on his way. "In their garage, at the end of the street," he said, almost as if his mouth had spoken the words without his brain's giving consent.

"Super!" Becca twirled the flashlight like a baton. "This whole job's going to be easy as pie."

Something bumped against Steve's arm, and he jerked. The paintbrush flew out of his hand, out of the narrow beam of light in which he worked, and disappeared in the surrounding darkness.

"Oh, it's you, Ginger." He breathed his relief and laid his hand on the head of his mother's orange tabby cat. She bumped her hard skull against his arm again and chirred, a sound deep in her throat, halfway between a mew and a purr. He scratched the length of her back, and tufts of fur hung in the air like dandelion seeds.

Becca had been standing over Steve, shining the flashlight along the surface of Donny's bike as he painted, and now she ran the flat beam over the grass.

"There it is," Steve said when he caught a flash of silver in the grass that would be the metal skirt on the brush.

Becca picked it up and handed it to him. "Are you almost done?" she asked. "I'm getting tired."

"I don't know. Shine the flashlight on it another time."

Becca ran the light methodically from one end of the large, balloon-tired bike to the other. In the darkness that preceded and followed the moving patch of light, the paint job looked dark and fine. In the circle of light it was streaked and blotchy.

Steve scratched his ear and another place on his elbow where a mosquito had gotten him, and he sighed. "I'm afraid it needs another coat."

"But that would be the third," Becca complained.

"I know. It's just not covering. It's like the paint doesn't stick. I don't know what's wrong."

"It'll look better when it dries." Becca had been saying that since he had finished the first coat.

"It had better," Steve said grimly. He started again with

the front fender, dipping the brush more deeply into the paint to lay on a thicker layer.

Still the paint seemed to sheet off, running down onto the tires and the rims and spokes, leaving the original blue and white design still showing through.

"Finished now?" Becca asked when he had worked his way around the reflector on the back fender for the third time.

"I guess so."

Becca shone the light again the length of the bike. "You'd better paint the handle grips."

"Nobody paints handle grips. Besides, they're rubber. I don't think you can paint rubber."

"But Celestino would have to do something with them. Like that they're a dead giveaway. The twins are the only kids on the block with such fancy handle grips. Maybe you should pull the red, white, and blue streamers out."

"No," Steve answered. "I'll paint the rubber." He knew how proud both Donny and Kenny were of those streamers.

When he was done Becca said again, "Don't worry. It'll look better tomorrow. Paint always looks like that when it's wet." Her voice sounded soothing, motherly, and Steve wanted to believe her.

"I hope so," he said.

He crammed the lid back onto the nearly empty paint can and wiped the brush on the grass. He needed paint thinner to clean the brush, but he hadn't thought of that before. He didn't want to risk rummaging around in the basement to find it. His parents would wake up and hear him for sure. He would just have to throw the brush away and hope his dad didn't come to him when he began looking for it. He stood up, his knees stiff and creaking. Ginger began rubbing against his ankles, twining between his legs, her purr thrumming in her throat.

"Now all we have to do is take this down to the garages and cover it some, so when the twins go by in the morning to get their bikes, it'll look like Celestino tried to hide it." Becca sounded like someone who was finishing off plans for a party.

"What'll the twins do when Celestino says he doesn't know anything about Donny's bike being behind his garage?" Steve was beginning to wish he had thought this whole idea through more carefully before he'd gone along with it. But even more, he wished he had never made up that story about Celestino's stealing bikes.

"Of course that's what he'll say. It's what he would say if he had taken it, too. Don't you see? They'll never believe him."

"I suppose not." Steve flipped the kick stand up with one foot and stood holding the bike by the handlebars. "Would you help?" he asked. "We have to get this thing parked behind Celestino's garage now."

"Sure." Becca walked around to the other side of the bike, took hold of the freshly painted handle grip, said "Yuck!" and wiped her hand on her shorts. She took a hold farther in, on the metal part of the handlebar, and commanded, "To the garage!" In her other hand she swung the flashlight so that the beam of light ran up a nearby tree and disappeared in the black sky.

Steve looked back at Ginger, who sat down on the edge of the lawn and washed her face. Steve could see the patch of white fur at her throat, bright in the moonlight.

Maybe Becca's right, he consoled himself. *Donny's bike will look better when the paint has dried.*

But when they had leaned the bike against the back of Celestino's garage and covered it lightly with branches torn from a nearby forsythia bush – not so much covering that the twins wouldn't see it – Steve knew that the bike would never look any better than it looked right then. And what it looked like then, as Becca ran the beam of light over it one last time, was a total disaster.

CHAPTER 5

Steve was dreaming. In the dream hundreds of bicycles pursued him wielding paintbrushes. The brushes dripped blood. He was fighting to get away, but every place he turned, one of the twins stood, barring his way and scowling. The bicycles were getting closer. They had Steve surrounded!

He jerked upright in bed, suppressing a scream.

"Oh, good. You're awake." It was his mother's voice.

Steve lifted one arm to shield his eyes from the penetrating morning light. He kicked at the sheet tangled around his legs.

His mother stood in the doorway of his room. She wiped her hands on her flowered apron and smiled. "Your father wants you to mow the lawn today, Steve. You'd better get at it before the day gets any hotter. It's going to be a scorcher again."

Ginger, who followed Steve's mother every place she went, was weaving in and out of her ankles, purring.

"Why me?" Steve complained, rubbing the grit from his eyes with a clenched fist. Sleepy seeds, his mother used to call it when he was little. "Dad never makes Matthew do the lawn anymore." One part of his brain was trying to reconstruct the dream that had thrust him into the morning so abruptly. The other part was trying to forget the whole thing, the dream and the twins and Donny's bike. Had they found it yet?

"Matthew had his turn mowing the lawn." Steve's mother said it cheerfully enough, but there was an edge to her voice the way there always was when anyone criticized Matthew.

Steve swung his legs out of the bed. "I don't see why he can't do it anyway. He's not working. He's not doing anything at all."

Ginger stalked across the room and leaped lightly onto Steve's rumpled bed. He petted her mechanically, and she arched her back beneath the stroking, increasing the volume of her purr and stiffening her tail so that it stood up straight and tickled Steve's nose.

A shadow seemed to settle on Steve's mother's face. She thrust a curling strand of gray hair out of her eyes abruptly. It failed to catch in the kerchief she wore to cover her hair when she was cleaning house, and tumbled back onto her forehead. "Now don't *you* start."

Steve stared at the floor sullenly, unable to meet his mother's gaze. "I just said Matthew never does anything around here anymore, and you know it's true."

"Matthew was pushing that mower when he was only eight years old," his mother said sharply. "He's done plenty of work around here. And besides" – her voice softened and she moved across the room to touch the foot of Steve's bed as though she wanted to touch him instead, but didn't dare – "we have to be patient, dear. We can't know what it was like for him, what he suffers. It must have been terrible . . . that war."

"Yeah," Steve said, in a voice that was patient about nothing.

His mother sighed, the air passing shrilly through compressed lips, the same way she always did when Steve's father complained about Matthew. "Just don't forget. Your father will expect to have the yard done when he comes home for lunch." She turned and left the room, and Ginger jumped down from the bed to follow.

"I know," Steve muttered, and he sat on the edge of his bed, staring at his dirty feet. There wasn't just dirt on them, there was red paint, too. It looked like dried blood. He remembered the dream again and a light shiver ran across his skin. He remembered last night, too, and that was worse than remembering the dream. When would he learn to keep his mouth shut so he didn't make trouble for himself and everybody around him?

Maybe it would work, though, if Donny really did blame Celestino when he found his bike. The hard part would be waiting for one of the twins to come by so he could find out what had happened.

He stood up and stretched, then inspected himself. There was paint on his hands, too, and some on his belly. There was even paint on a mosquito bite on one elbow. He wondered if his mother had noticed. No. She was too busy worrying about her soldier boy to notice anything about Steve. He walked over to his dresser and took a pair of brown socks and a light-blue T-shirt out of the top drawer.

The twins always went shirtless in the summer. Most of the

boys did, except Celestino . . . and Steve. Steve wore a shirt because he had redhead skin that sunburned and freckled but never tanned. Also, he wore a shirt because he felt fatter without one. He wondered what Celestino was hiding beneath his T-shirt. Maybe he had a heart and a snake and a naked girl tattooed on his chest. No. If Celestino had a naked girl tattooed on his chest, he would go bare-chested for sure.

Steve found his blue jeans crumpled in one corner. They were paint-spattered, too. He kicked that pair under his bed and got a clean pair out of his drawer. He would have to find the paint remover, get those dirty jeans cleaned up.

He went into the bathroom and bent over the brown marble sink, scrubbing his hands with a nail brush until most of the paint was gone and his skin was red and raw.

Dumb paint. It was on everything. And then Steve thought . . . *everything!* He had cleaned the paintbrush in the grass the night before. How could he have been so stupid? Celestino would come by, or the twins. One of them would see the grass, and then everyone would know.

The grass clippings made an arching spray in the air that fell just short of Steve's feet. He leaned into the mower, his head lowered, his elbows straight, pushing from the shoulders. The heat from the sun was like a pressure against the back of his neck and his shoulders.

Steve stopped and studied the patch of grass where he and Becca had painted the bike, where he had wiped the brush. He had mowed it first until there wasn't a bit of red anywhere, not a single blade showing any paint. Then he had done most of the rest of the yard and come back to go over this small corner again.

He wiped his hands on his jeans. Good thing his mother had made him do the grass this morning. If he'd thought of the paint and started mowing on his own, she would have known he'd been up to something for sure. So one thing had worked out right anyway. Maybe the rest would follow.

Steve sniffed. The cut grass smelled like summer. He wondered if anyone had ever tried to bottle that smell for perfume. Fresh-cut grass and baking bread; they had to be the two best smells in the world. He settled into mowing once more. The mower whirred, then clattered when he pulled it back to start again.

The hens, inside their fence, were clucking softly to themselves, scratching and pecking busily in the dust of the chicken yard. The rooster moved among them, his head high, his wattles vibrating with self-importance. Steve turned the mower and ran it toward them, pulling it back abruptly in the instant before it banged into the fence. A couple of the hens hopped, half-flew away from the fence, squawking, and the rooster ruffled his neck feathers and turned to face the invader. Steve chuckled without amusement and turned the mower back, pushing it along the side of the garden.

He was following the small strip of grass that separated the garden from the alley when he saw Celestino sauntering down the alley toward him; his thumbs were hooked in the pockets of his blue jeans. Again he was wearing a T-shirt with the sleeves rolled to show off his muscles. Steve tightened his grip on the mower and lowered his head, concentrating on the fragrant shower of grass clippings.

To Steve's surprise, when Celestino drew close he stepped onto the next patch of grass the mower was aimed for. "Hi," he said, his voice neutral, almost friendly.

Steve stopped pushing the mower. "Hi," he answered, and then he waited for whatever Celestino would say next.

Celestino hooked his thumbs more deeply into the pockets of his jeans. "You gonna be done with your work pretty soon?"

"Yeah. I guess so." Steve glanced at Celestino's face and dropped his gaze again. "What's it to you?"

"I thought you might wanna do something when you're done."

Steve tried to lean casually against the mower, but it inched forward toward Celestino's feet with a slight whir. Celestino didn't move. "Why should I?" Steve asked, and the question, which was meant to be tough, came out sounding as if he actually wanted a reason.

"You ain't still mad about yesterday, are you?"

Steve didn't know what to say to that. It seemed as if yesterday out at the foxhole had been a hundred years ago. He didn't *feel* mad. He didn't feel anything but worried about Donny and his bike. "I suppose not," he answered, avoiding looking at Celestino's face.

"Then you wanna go out to the foxhole and mess around?"

Celestino inviting him out to his own foxhole! Steve could feel the heat rising to his face, but he answered, "I think my father might have something else he wants me to do."

"Your dad's at work," Celestino said. It wasn't a threat. Just a simple statement, but heavy with implication.

Steve tried to force a small chuckle. "He leaves orders with my mother," he explained, reaching for the understanding all boys share about father's orders.

"Yeah?" It wasn't really a question, though it was spoken as one. It was also spoken like someone who didn't submit to orders, not even from a father.

Steve resumed his mowing, and Celestino stepped aside. "The twins going to be there?" Steve asked, bending heavily over the handle of the mower and pushing with a great thrust.

"No," Celestino replied.

"No?"

Celestino's mouth smiled, but his eyes were as dark and unamused as bits of coal. "No. The twins ain't gonna be there."

Steve flexed his hands to relieve his cramped muscles. He didn't say anything. There didn't seem to be anything to say.

He turned the corner by the other side of the garden and began pushing the mower away from Celestino, though he had already mowed that part of the yard. Maybe Becca's idea had worked. Maybe the twins were mad at Celestino. But if they were, why hadn't they come by before now?

"It'll be a while before I can come," he said. "Next I have to rake."

"That's okay. I'll wait." Celestino hunkered down, picking up a cut blade of grass and placing it deliberately between his teeth.

Steve walked the mower to the house, opened the outside cellar doors, and bumped the machine slowly down the concrete steps. In the cool darkness of the basement he paused and wiped the sweat from his forehead onto his shirt sleeve. He supported himself for a moment against the rough wall. What did Celestino want with him anyway? Surely he didn't expect to be friends with someone he had just been calling names the day before. Maybe he would get tired of waiting. Steve reached for the rake. He didn't ordinarily rake the lawn after he mowed it, but this time it was going to be raked until every blade of grass stood at attention. He got a bushel basket to put the clippings in.

Emerging onto the lawn, carrying basket and rake, he could see that Celestino was running his fingers back and forth through the grass. If he was looking for evidence, he wasn't going to find it where he was. But then Celestino wouldn't have any reason to be looking, would he? Even if he suspected Steve, he had no way of knowing that just a little while before there had been paint clearly visible in the grass.

When Steve had the basket full of grass clippings, he stood over it, considering. In the fall, they always dumped the raked leaves at the curb in front of the house and burned them. Steve doubted that grass clippings would burn, and he had a feeling his father wouldn't appreciate finding them in the street.

"I have to carry this to the woods," he called to Celestino, who had remained sitting where he was, sifting through the loose grass, apparently with perfect patience.

"You done here?" Celestino asked, getting up.

"Not quite. I still have to do the back part of the yard. You're probably getting tired of waiting."

"Not me." Again the smile. "Here. I'll take the basket, then you can finish raking. Save time." Celestino stood facing Steve, holding out his hands.

"Uh . . . sure." There was nothing Steve could do but relinquish the basket. "It won't take me a whole lot longer, unless" – he paused significantly – "there's something more my dad told my mother I'm supposed to do."

"Doesn't matter," Celestino said, balancing the basket on one shoulder and starting down the alley toward the woods. "I got nothing better to do."

Steve finished the raking slowly. The grass clippings filled another half-basket. When he was doing the corner of the yard behind the chicken pen, he couldn't help looking for signs of paint, but he didn't find any. He had done that part so thoroughly that he had apparently chopped the clippings too small for any sign to remain.

"I'll have to check with my mom now," he said when Celestino returned from emptying the half-basket.

Celestino nodded, folded his arms across his chest, and proceeded to wait. Steve carried the bushel basket and the rake into the basement, pulling the slanting cellar doors closed behind himself. He climbed the inside stairs to the kitchen. His mother was there, kneading bread dough on a floury board on the kitchen table.

The yeasty smell of the raw dough and the tuneless melody his mother hummed as she worked suddenly made Steve's knees feel rubbery. He wanted with his whole being to be small again, the size he was when he could crawl into her lap. But that was ridiculous . . . of course. After all, what could Celestino do? Maybe he did only want someone to mess around with.

Steve didn't believe it for a minute.

He closed the basement door, and his mother looked up, already smiling. "So," she said, "you've finished the mowing. You really did a good job of it. I saw you out there, raking away."

Steve stared at the sprigs of flowers in the linoleum on the kitchen floor and mumbled, "Thanks."

"Your father will be pleased," she added.

"Is there anything else you need me to do?" he asked.

Her eyebrows lifted in surprise, so he amended his question.

"I mean, I don't have anything else to do. I'd be glad . . . if I could help."

"Didn't I see that new boy, Ray Celestino, with you?"

"Oh, yeah. He's hanging around. But I don't think he really wants to play. He's two years older than me. He starts high school in the fall, you know." Steve pulled off a bit of the bread dough she was working and popped it into his mouth.

"I saw him with the twins yesterday. They're your age. I'm sure there's no boys in the neighborhood closer to his age than you three."

"Yeah . . . probably. But still . . . if there's anything else you need . . ."

She formed the dough into a large ball, plopped it into a greased bowl, turned it once, and covered the bowl with a dish towel. She shook her head. "That's lovely of you, dear, but you've done enough. Why don't you run along and play now? I'm sure that's what Ray came over here for."

"Sure," Steve said. "I'll just bet it is," and he turned and shuffled toward the back door. He could see Celestino, still waiting, though what he was waiting for was difficult to imagine. Steve wondered how he could get rid of him and go to look up the twins. He wondered, too, why even Becca hadn't shown up this morning. Where did everybody disappear to when you needed a friend?

CHAPTER 6

"Your girlfriend coming over to play today?" Celestino walked down the alley in the direction of the woods with long, loose strides.

Steve tried to keep the irritation out of his voice. "Becca? She's not my girlfriend. She's just . . . a friend. I've been friends with her – and the twins – since we were little."

They had reached the path through the alfalfa field and Celestino stopped at the point the path took off from the alley. "Let's go get her."

Steve studied Celestino's face. "Why? Why do you want Becca?"

Celestino gave an elaborate shrug. "An army needs lots of soldiers."

"I don't know if she'll want to play army."

"Let's go see." Celestino had already started on the path that led to Becca's house and the mill, and there didn't seem to be anything to do but follow.

They found Becca sitting in the canopied glider swing in

her side yard reading a Nancy Drew book. It was a new one, *Mystery of the Tolling Bell.*

"Hi," Celestino said.

"Hi," Steve echoed, feeling stupid, feeling like a marionette with Celestino pulling his strings.

Becca glanced from Celestino to Steve and back to Celestino again. "Hi," she said coolly, then she returned to her book.

Steve admired her composure. She didn't look startled, even when she first saw Celestino.

"You wanna be in my army?" Celestino asked.

Becca lowered her book slowly. "Is Steve in it?"

"Sure."

Steve could feel the sheepish grin that had taken residence on his face.

"What about the twins?" she asked. She was avoiding looking at Steve.

"Nah. They're out. They don't want to play no more."

Becca slipped a bookmark in between the pages and closed her book. "Why's that? I thought you and the twins were real buddies."

Steve held his breath, waiting for the answer to the question he had been afraid to ask. Over by the mill, freight cars banged together with a crack like close thunder. The sound seemed to penetrate his skin.

Celestino turned his palms out, lifted his shoulders. "I don't feel like hanging around with those guys today. Is that okay?"

Becca looked at Steve then, and her face glowed with suppressed satisfaction. But where were the twins, Steve wondered, if their plan had worked?

"Come on," Celestino said. "Let's go." Becca laid down

her book, and both Becca and Steve followed Celestino into the woods.

They walked silently, single file, Celestino in the lead. *On our way to* Celestino's *foxhole,* Steve thought grimly. He could have kicked himself for getting into such a stupid situation. He kept looking for an opportunity to tell Celestino that he didn't want to play, that he wanted to go home, but there never seemed to be a time he could do anything but go along. He had thought Becca would find an excuse, perhaps for both of them, but she wasn't being any help at all. And here he was, going to "play army" with Celestino. He wondered what the older boy really had in mind. He wasn't worried, though. If it came to a fight, it would be two against one. Becca was a pretty good partner in a pinch.

They slid down into a ravine, jumped a creek, and clambered up the other side, avoiding a patch of poison ivy. At least Steve avoided it. Becca and Celestino walked right through the middle. Becca wasn't allergic to poison ivy. Steve hoped that Celestino was. Tomorrow, when Celestino was home scratching, Steve would have a chance to check out the twins.

The woods were not as hot as the sunny yards, but still the trees held back any trace of a breeze, and the air was stifling. The silence that surrounded the trek was different from the kind of woods silence Steve and his friends usually moved in. Steve found himself glancing occasionally over his shoulder. There was nothing to see but the familiar intertwined trees and the thin, leaf-filtered light.

When they got to the clearing where the foxhole was, Celestino stepped aside, letting Steve and Becca move on ahead. The noon sun was nearly straight above them. Gnats swarmed around Steve's head. He flapped at them with both hands, but they were undisturbed, returning immediately to hang in the heavy air directly in front of his eyes.

Steve and Becca moved through the long grass in what seemed to Steve like a kind of slow motion, as if they were walking through something thicker than air, something congealed and gummy. He wished he could speak to Becca, ask for her ideas about getting rid of Celestino, but there was no opportunity. And with Celestino there, he could hardly look at her without being afraid he would give himself away.

They had almost reached the edge of the foxhole when the attack came.

It began with a blow that caught Steve just between the shoulder blades. He twisted to defend himself, but he saw Becca going down. She fell like a sack of flour, right into the foxhole. He turned back, tried to reach for her, but in that instant there was another, lighter blow, just behind his knees, and he was pitching forward. His hands reached out, grabbing nothing but air, and the instant of falling was like the endless, floating fall in a nightmare. He had time for several thoughts, it seemed, while space rushed past him. But the only one he could remember when he hit the solid clay of the bottom of the foxhole was *I knew it. I knew he'd get us.*

At the impact of the fall, Steve's stomach lurched, and a wave of heat passed through him that was almost nausea. He lay there for a second, struggling for breath and sense. He hadn't imagined that Celestino could be so strong, so quick, to get them both at once.

"What're you trying to do?" he yelled. "Kill us? You might have broken somebody's neck with that trick." Steve scrambled to his feet and turned, ready to take Celestino on, with or without Becca's help. But it wasn't Celestino who looked down on him from the edge of the foxhole. It was Kenny and Donny Riley.

"That'd be okay," Donny said quietly. "I wouldn't mind."

Steve could feel his knees turning to liquid. The twins knew. Somehow they knew. But how?

Becca was on her feet now, demanding, "What do you guys want with us?"

Neither of the twins replied. Celestino had moved up behind them now and stood there, looking over the tops of their heads, but he didn't say anything either. And the twins stood, studying Steve and Becca, their eyes sky-blue, dark-fringed, their brown hair standing in erratic tufts that seemed to point in several directions at once.

"What do you *think* they want?" Celestino sneered.

"How should we know?" Becca's fists were cocked on her hips. She seemed the picture of injured innocence. Steve's tongue was glued to the roof of his mouth, and he kept flushing hot and cold.

"You wanna show them, Riley?" Celestino said. It was more of an order than a question.

Without a word, Donny turned and walked into the woods, returning a moment later, pushing his bicycle.

Becca had been wrong. The bike had not improved as the paint dried. If anything, it looked worse than it had looked in the night. The paint was streaked and blotched, so thin in some places that the original blue and white showed clearly as through an uneven red film, so thick in others that it had obviously not dried. Bits of grass and dirt were stuck to the bike, embedded in the paint. Some leaves from the cover they used had stuck, too. The tires, the rims, and the wheel spokes were paint-spattered. Even the black seat had smudges that looked like red fingerprints on it. The handle grips were black and red, and enough of the paint had run down the red, white, and blue streamers to have glued them into a single, muddled string.

"What was the big idea?" Kenny demanded.

"Yeah," Donny seconded. "What'd I ever do to you guys?" He was trying to sound tough, but the corners of his mouth were jerking as if he might start crying at any moment. Steve couldn't look at either the bike or the boy holding it.

"Why are you asking us?" Becca asked, still trying to stall.

"Because you did it. Steve and you," Kenny replied.

"Says who?" She took a step backward to the other side of the foxhole, but her voice was on the attack. "Why would we want to paint Donny's bike?" Steve wished she would be quiet. He was feeling sick to his stomach again.

"Yeah. Why would you?" Donny's jaw was tight, and he pushed the bike closer to the edge of the foxhole as if he meant to ram someone in the chest with it.

Celestino moved forward, stepping between the twins so he was balanced on the edge of the foxhole. "Why don't matter. I can prove you did."

"Then prove it!" Becca said, crossing her arms over her chest.

"First," Celestino said, standing over them like a master of ceremonies, "I'll show you how we caught you out, Hansen."

Becca didn't say anything. She sniffed, tilting her already pug nose a little higher in the air.

"Turn the bike around, Riley."

Donny obediently turned the bike the other way.

"See them prints?" Celestino pointed to the perfect shape of a curled hand formed in the red paint on one handle grip. "That's a girl's hand."

"Oh, come on," Becca scoffed. "You can't tell if it's a boy or a girl from a handprint." But she uncrossed her arms and held her hands behind her back as she spoke. Steve glanced over at her and could see the remains of red paint on one palm. She hadn't scrubbed as hard as he had. Celestino had probably checked that out when he first saw her. So the jig was up – for Becca anyway.

"And there's more." Celestino pulled a blue bandanna out of his back pocket and unfolded it carefully. "See this?" He held something up between his index finger and thumb. Steve squinted and moved closer. The sunlight caught what Celestino was holding, and Steve could begin to make it out. It was a tuft of short, orange-yellow hair. He reached up to touch his own reddish hair, but Celestino shook his head. "Afraid you lost a curl, Pulaski?" he asked. "This ain't human hair." Steve leaned forward for another look.

"What is it, then?" Becca asked. She hadn't moved from where she stood or unclasped her hands from behind her back.

Celestino drew himself up, holding the evidence higher. "It's cat hair, can't you tell? It's hair from an orange cat. I found it stuck to the paint."

"So?"

Steve knew what Becca was doing; she was playing dumb, waiting for Celestino to lay out all his proof so she could counter it. He also knew it wouldn't do any good. They were caught.

Celestino narrowed his eyes until they were dark glints. "So . . . whose ma has an orange cat?"

"Ginger?" Becca scoffed. "You can't prove that hair is from Ginger, and even if you could, she's all over the neighborhood. She might have brushed up against the bike anywhere."

"Anywhere," Celestino repeated. "Like in Pulaski's backyard."

"You can't prove that." If pure stubbornness could win an argument, Becca would never lose.

Celestino smirked. "Can't I? Then what about this?" And he reached carefully into the bandanna and removed another object, cupping it in his hand.

"What's that?" Steve asked, beginning to grow intrigued with the case that was being made, even if it was against him.

For a moment Celestino held whatever he had as if he wasn't going to show it, looking down on Steve and Becca. Then he crouched and thrust the new evidence directly in front of their faces.

"It's only some grass," Becca said.

"You're right." Celestino's smile beamed with benevolence. He might have been a teacher praising a slow student for her first correct answer. "Grass . . . from Pulaski's backyard . . . from behind the chicken coop. I saw it there early this morning, right after I talked to the twins." He laid a clump of grass, the dirt still clinging to its roots, in his hand and turned it gently with the tip of a dirty finger. "All covered with red paint."

Steve moved forward to see if what Celestino said was true. It was. The red paint didn't really look red against the green, more black or dark gray, but the grass was clearly painted, and Steve knew it to be red, however the color might look.

"You thought you was smart, mowing your grass this morning."

"It doesn't look like red paint to me," Becca said. "But even if it is, anybody could have brought Donny's bike to Steve's yard, painted it, then hidden it behind Celestino's garage. What makes them think you didn't do it, Celestino?"

Steve understood what Becca had done before anyone had reacted. No one had mentioned where the bike had been found. She had just given them away. Steve was filled with something close to exhilaration, relief. He was glad to have it over.

Celestino's teeth flashed. "What did you say? You wanna say it again, Hansen?"

Steve turned to look at Becca. Her glance slid from one corner of the foxhole to another, and her face was bright crimson. She knew, too.

"I mean," she said, "I just assume that's where Donny found his bike, behind Celestino's garage."

No one was listening to Becca anymore. They had all they needed to know from her. The three of them were staring at Steve, their eyes like X-rays that saw right through to the bone, eyes that saw his guilt as if it were printed for them to read.

"Okay," Steve admitted. "I did it. I painted Donny's bike and hid it behind Celestino's garage . . . for you to find."

"Why?" Donny asked, his voice barely more than a whisper.

"Because I wanted you to be mad at Celestino," Steve admitted. "I thought you would think he had stolen it and was going to sell it. And I wanted you to come back and be my friends." And then, to his own amazement, he began to bawl.

CHAPTER 7

Steve sat on the bottom of the foxhole, his ankles tied, his hands behind his back lashed to Becca's wrists. Becca was sitting the same way, her back to him, her ankles tied in front of her.

Steve's tears had stopped almost as abruptly as they had begun, but he hadn't fought much when the twins had tied him under Celestino's orders. Now he was left with nothing but his mortification. Becca had fought so fiercely it had taken all three of them to subdue her, and now, twenty minutes after the others had disappeared into the woods, she was still struggling futilely against the bonds.

"Becca," Steve said sharply. "Why don't you settle down? You're making my back hurt."

Becca's wrenching jerks quieted, and for several moments neither of them spoke. Steve sighed and let his weight sink back against hers. From his position in the bottom of the foxhole he couldn't see anything but the tops of trees and a patch of sky decorated with a plume of white smoke from the mill stack. There was nothing to hear but woods' sounds: a squirrel scolding in a nearby tree, the endless rustling of leaves, a crow giving its warning cry somewhere in the distance. He wondered if Celestino or the twins would come back for them . . . ever. He didn't suppose they would. Donny might have if it hadn't been his bike they'd ruined.

Matthew ought to be able to figure out where to find them, if he cared enough to come looking. It was Matthew who had discovered this clearing when he was still a kid. He used to bring Steve out here, filled him with stories about its being magic, a kind of fairy circle.

Stories. Steve was never going to tell a story again as long as he lived. They were nothing but trouble. Pure trouble.

"Steve?" Becca spoke very quietly.

"Yes?"

"Are you mad at me?"

"Why would I be mad at you?"

"Because the whole dumb thing was my idea. You know it was."

Steve stopped to consider. Was he mad at Becca? What good did it do to be mad at someone you were tied up with? "No," he said finally. "It's my fault more than yours. I'm the one who painted it, and nobody held a gun to my head." He was the one who had made up the story about Celestino stealing bikes, too, but he wasn't going to say that.

Becca was quiet for a long time. Finally she said, "Do you remember the time I did that experiment with the marbles?"

"You mean when you let your whole bag of nibs loose on the floor in the middle of the horror movie?"

"From the very back of the theater," she added, and then she didn't say any more.

"What about it?" Steve asked finally.

"The manager threw you out . . . you and the twins, but he didn't say a word to me. He didn't even ask if I had anything to do with it."

"Yeah. I know. So what?"

"I was just thinking. . . . I'm awfully sorry."

"You're sorry about the marbles in the theater . . . now?"

"Uh-huh. And about the time I set the fire in the middle of the railroad tracks."

"I remember that," Steve said, getting into the spirit of Becca's apology. "You wanted to see how fast the switch engines going to the mill could stop."

"And the fireman from the engine caught you instead of me."

"You run faster." But Steve could still remember the feel of the fireman's rough gloves on the back of his neck. Becca had come back and confessed, and the man wouldn't believe she had anything to do with it.

"He called you a hooligan and shook you until I could hear your teeth clicking together like . . . those things Spanish dancers wear on their fingers."

"Castanets," Steve said.

"Yeah."

A fly crawled across Steve's face, and he twitched his nose, trying to make it go away.

"What I'm really thinking," Becca explained slowly, "is that at least this time I'm taking the rap with you. I'm glad for that."

"I guess I'm glad, too," Steve said, watching the fly drone back and forth in front of his eyes. "I wouldn't much like to be tied out here all alone."

Becca was quiet then with whatever her thoughts were, and Steve sat listening to the buzzing heat. He wondered how long it would take his mother to convince his father that he might be in trouble and that they should begin to search. His father's philosophy was that boys were probably into some mischief during most of their waking hours but that the one thing you didn't need to worry about was their coming home. "Their stomachs will bring them home soon enough, Molly," he would say. "A boy's stomach can always find his way home for him." Steve's stomach rumbled menacingly at the thought of his father's certainty.

Becca began to giggle.

"What's so funny?" Steve demanded.

"I was just thinking about those marbles."

"Yeah? What about them? I never could understand why anybody would throw away perfectly good nibs like that. A lot of them were mine, too. I was going to win them back."

"But it was worth it, Steve. You know it was."

"What are you talking about?"

"Just to see them . . . the kids . . . popping out of their seats the way they did . . . jumping up, screaming . . . all the way down to the front of the theater!" Becca laughed.

Steve sighed, thinking *Maybe this will seem funny someday, too,* but he couldn't believe that it would. He couldn't imagine the thought of Donny's ruined bike or days – and nights – tied in the bottom of a foxhole ever seeming funny.

"Why did the Little Moron salute the refrigerator?"

Steve groaned. "Not another one. You've been telling those dumb jokes for hours. Nobody in the world knows as many Little Moron jokes as you do."

Becca shifted her position. Steve could feel the bones in her spine. They seemed to match exactly with his spine so that the little knobs grated against one another every time she moved. She didn't say anything.

Steve waited for a while and finally said, "Go ahead. You might as well finish it."

"Finish what?" Becca's voice was all innocence.

"The joke! The joke you were telling."

"What joke?"

"Why did the Little Moron salute the refrigerator?"

"Don't you know?"

"Of course I don't know. I would have answered you if I knew."

"Because it was General Electric." Becca was off in a fit of giggling. Steve groaned.

They had been sitting for hours. Steve's wrists and ankles hurt where they were tied, and his back ached, between his shoulder blades especially, and his knees were stiff, and his neck was in knots, and his tailbone seemed to be burrowing into the clay. And besides all that, his bladder was about to burst.

The sun had disappeared from their small patch of sky;

the four-o'clock mill whistle had blown to signal a change of shifts; the shadows from the trees had stretched their cooling fingers across the foxhole. And the mosquitoes had arrived.

There were always insects in the summer woods, of course, and Steve had sat for a while with considerable interest watching a bright red daddy longlegs make its way down one side of the foxhole, across his legs, and up the other. With the first touch of shade, though, the mosquitoes came with a vengeance. They hummed next to Steve's ears for maddening minutes while selecting a place to bite, the tender flesh of his throat or the knobby knuckle of one thumb. They bit through his shirt and in his scalp. And of course, with his hands tied he was helpless to swat or scratch. He remembered a Tarzan movie he had seen where Tarzan rescued a man staked out over a hill of man-eating ants. Could man-eating ants possibly be worse than kid-eating mosquitoes?

"Shall we yell some more?" Becca asked.

"What good does it do? You know we're too far away for anybody to hear."

"Maybe Matthew will hear us. He spends a lot of time in the woods."

"Only when he doesn't have anything else to do," Steve snapped, and Becca fell silent again.

They sat without speaking for some time. Cicadas were shrilling in the trees all around them, a steady, high-pitched drone that drowned out every other sound. When Steve closed his eyes he could imagine it was the sound of an army of ants discussing tender kids for dinner, moving closer.

"Railroad crossing, watch for cars. Can you spell that without any *r*'s?"

Steve jerked his bobbing head. "What? What'd you say?"

Becca repeated the riddle. "Railroad crossing, watch for cars. Can you spell that without any *r*'s?"

"Of course not. And you can't either." Steve bent forward and tried to rub his nose against his knees, but the small mound of his belly and the ropes that attached him so tightly to Becca prevented him from reaching. It seemed to him that noses never itched except when you were in a position that made it impossible to scratch.

"Yes I can," Becca insisted.

"Go ahead, then."

"T-H-A-T! That! Get it?"

There was nothing to do but groan again. Becca took it as appreciation. Appreciation always silenced her for a few minutes.

Before she could start up again, Steve said mournfully, "I'll bet they've all finished supper by now."

"Yeah." He could feel Becca nodding her head. "You're probably right."

"How much longer do you think it'll be before your mother begins worrying about you?" Steve asked.

"You mean really worrying so she'll send somebody out to look or just fretting?"

"So she'll send somebody out to look."

"Not very soon, I don't think. She wouldn't worry at lunchtime. She'd figure I got a sandwich at your house. And we've been late for supper so many times that she'll be cross I'm not there, but I don't think she'd worry – not until later."

"Same here," Steve said. And after a moment he added, "I wish we'd been better about getting to supper on time, then we'd know they were looking." He rubbed his cheek on his shoulder, trying to scratch a clump of mosquito bites. They only itched more furiously with the rubbing.

"We've even missed 'The Lone Ranger,'" Becca mourned. "I'll bet nobody turned on the radio so we can find out what happened."

"We've missed lunch and supper, too." Steve's stomach had long since quit rumbling and gone to little whining shrieks.

"What if we're out here all night?" Becca asked, her voice sounding a little tremulous for the first time.

"We won't be. Somebody will find us before then." Steve tried to sound very sure of himself. Somehow Becca's being worried – even a little – made it easier for him to feel strong.

"Can we yell again?"

"Okay. Sure." Not that it would do any good.

Becca took a deep breath, tipped her head back so that Steve's chin was forced down onto his chest, and yelled "HELP!" Steve added his voice to hers but there was no response, except for the silence of the woods.

"Wait . . . listen!" Steve commanded.

They both held their breaths, listening.

"What do you hear?" Becca whispered after a moment.

"Nothing. It's just that the woods got so quiet." They both listened, and then Steve added, relief coloring his voice, "I know what it is. The cicadas have quit."

"Maybe we scared them."

"Well . . . at least there's something afraid of us, even if it is bugs."

Becca giggled, but long after the giggle stopped, Steve could still feel her shoulders shake. He knew she was crying, but he didn't say anything. He didn't want to embarrass her. After all, she hadn't said anything when he had bawled.

It was nearly dark in the clearing when Steve suddenly sat up straighter, jerking his head up from a near doze. "What was that?" he whispered.

"What was what?" Becca asked.

"I don't know. I heard something. At least I think I did. Something's different, anyway."

They both sat perfectly still, straining for the smallest sound. There was nothing.

"I know what it is!" Steve whispered after a moment. "The cicadas are quiet again."

"Maybe they've just gone to sleep," Becca suggested. "I suppose cicadas sleep, too, don't they?"

Steve didn't know whether they did or not, but he sat at attention, straining for the slightest sound. The silence of the night woods bore down on him with a suffocating weight. He could hear each breath Becca took. She sucked at the air and let it go again in ragged bursts. He could hear the pounding of his own heart as well.

And then he heard a twig snap, the soft slap of a branch being pushed aside and allowed to spring into place, and a light stabbed him in the face, blinding him, making it impossible for him to see anything at all.

"There you are. I might have guessed." Matthew played the light back and forth across Steve and Becca and added, "My God! Are you tied?"

"No," Steve replied, striving for just the right air of jauntiness and soldierly unconcern. "We stayed out here because we got tired of eating."

CHAPTER 8

After struggling with the great assortment of knots for a few minutes, Matthew took out a pocket knife and began sawing through the bonds.

"I'll bet the twins are going to be in trouble," Becca said. "This is probably their mother's clothesline."

Matthew didn't say anything. He simply went on sawing at the rope with his knife. When one part of the rope fell away, he began again, fiercely, on another, and soon Steve and Becca were both released. But being released and standing up were two entirely different things. Steve discovered that his knees wouldn't straighten out, and when Matthew helped Becca to walk to the edge of the foxhole, Steve capsized like a turtle upended and left to roll helplessly onto its back.

Matthew returned to him, bent over him, wordlessly helped him to the edge of the foxhole next to Becca, and massaged his legs until the cramped muscles and tight joints began to ease a little. Steve could just see Matthew's face in the last traces of shadowy light. There was anger in the set of Matthew's jaw, but great gentleness in his hands.

"The twins, you say? They did this to you?"

"And Celestino," Becca added. "Celestino was behind the whole thing."

Steve shot her a warning look. She would be telling Matthew about painting Donny's bike next. But she wasn't paying any attention to him.

"Did you know," she was saying to Matthew as he began rubbing her legs, "that Celestino steals bikes . . . steals them and paints them and sells them to the Mafia in Chicago?"

"Steals bikes and sells them to the Mafia?" Matthew murmured as he stood up. "Sounds pretty serious." He was talking to Becca, but he was looking at Steve as he spoke.

Steve could feel himself flushing. "I didn't say for sure he sold them to the Mafia," he said, knowing how silly the story sounded in Matthew's ears. "I just said maybe he did. He comes from Chicago, you know," he concluded lamely, speaking now directly to Matthew.

"So he steals bikes?" Matthew inquired softly.

"Sure. All the kids from Chicago are thieves. Everybody knows that." The burning heat had traveled to Steve's scalp now.

"Be careful, Steve," Matthew warned. "Sometimes what 'everybody knows' isn't worth knowing."

"But Steve saw him," Becca explained urgently. "He saw him back behind his garage one night, painting a stolen bike, a *girl's* bike." It was apparent that in Becca's eyes the bike's being identified as a girl's increased the crime tenfold.

"Did you, Steve?" Matthew's gaze was unwavering, and Steve cleared his throat and scraped his heels against the side of the foxhole. He didn't usually have any trouble answering questions. In fact, answers to difficult questions usually popped into his head without any effort on his part. But there was something about the steady way Matthew stood there that made each reply that came to his mind die unspoken.

"He did!" Becca exclaimed. "He told me."

But Matthew was still standing in front of Steve, waiting for an answer.

No more stories, Steve warned himself sternly, but his tongue seemed to have a mind of its own. "Well," he said, "I thought that was what Celestino was doing when I saw him . . . painting a bike. It was dark, though, behind the garages . . . hard to tell for sure."

Matthew's forehead furrowed and his eyebrows met in a continuous line.

"What do you mean?" Becca demanded. "You *thought* that was what he was doing? You told me you saw him. You told me Celestino stole bikes!"

"Yes. He probably does." Steve turned his head so he didn't have to look at Matthew, but in turning away from Matthew he was faced with Becca. Even in the dim light he could see the way she was puffed up, partly with indignation, partly with mosquito bites.

"Probably. Probably!" Her voice rose to an enraged squeak. "You told me, Stephen Pulaski. You told me you saw. We stole Donny's bike and painted it because you *said* Celestino did it all the time, that he would get blamed for sure."

Steve lowered his head into his hands. Now Matthew knew everything. He might as well have told the truth himself from the very beginning. At least he could have gotten credit then for coming clean.

"It sounds like you two have some accounting to do tomorrow," Matthew said, not unkindly, and he helped Becca to her feet. When he reached for Steve's arm, Steve stood up quickly on his own. He didn't need any help.

Matthew let the hand he had reached toward Steve fall to his side, awkwardly. "Does Donny have his bike back now?" he asked.

Steve nodded.

"He has it back," Becca announced, her tone self-righteous, as if she had had nothing to do with the whole thing, "but it's ruined. Steve painted it red, and he really botched it."

"*I* painted it red?" Steve exclaimed. "I'd like to know whose idea it was in the first place. I'd like to know who kept saying it would look fine after it dried."

Becca leaned forward, her hands on her hips, her teeth flashing in the gathering darkness. "And I'd like to know who made up that whole story about Celestino stealing bikes. I should have figured it was a lie. That's all you are, Steve, a big, fat liar, and I should have known."

"Who are you calling fat?" Steve took a step toward Becca, his fists clenched, but Matthew put a restraining hand against Steve's chest.

"Skinny. Fat. I don't care," Becca shouted. "You're a liar!"

"Okay," Matthew soothed. "Simmer down. No use getting mad at each other. It strikes me you two have enough other people put out with both of you. You'd better stick together."

Becca crossed her arms over her chest and turned her back on Steve. Steve stuffed his still-clenched fists into his pockets and kicked at the side of the foxhole. Every place he turned in the last couple of days, people were calling him names.

"So you painted Donny's bike, huh? And it didn't come out too well," Matthew said.

"It looks terrible," Becca supplied.

"Especially after it dried," Steve tossed out in Becca's direction.

"I thought Donny was your friend?" Matthew said. It was more a question than a statement of something Matthew thought.

"He is," Steve replied, and then added miserably, "He was. I didn't mean to ruin his bike. I only wanted him to be mad at Celestino. I figured he'd think Celestino had done it."

Matthew nodded as if he understood, but Steve wondered if anybody could really understand. The whole thing sounded so dumb now. He wondered how he ever could have gone along with Becca's idea.

"We'd better go," Matthew said. "You kids have two sets of worried parents at home."

The walk back through the woods was slow. Night waited for them beneath the trees, a living thing that opened up and swallowed them as they left the clearing. Matthew's flashlight illuminated only one step at a time. Looming phantoms crowded in from every side and closed behind them as they walked. Most places there wasn't room to walk three abreast, so Becca moved on ahead, her nose pointed so high in the air that it was surprising she could see to walk. Matthew followed, trying to pick out a path for her with the flashlight, a path that she ignored. Steve wondered why Matthew bothered.

Steve had to go to the bathroom really badly now, but he wasn't about to ask the other two to stop and wait while he went off into the blackened woods. Not that he was afraid of the woods at night, but if Becca didn't have to go, he wasn't going to admit he had to. Besides, Becca was probably mad enough to make some kind of embarrassing remark. There didn't seem to be anybody left in the world who wasn't mad at him.

He walked close behind Matthew, very close behind. He remembered hanging on to Matthew's belt when he was small – catching a ride, as he used to call it – and it was all he could do to keep from reaching out and grabbing his brother's belt now. *Wait*, he wanted to say. *Don't you be mad, too. I didn't mean to lie.*

He didn't say it, though. If Matthew didn't need him, he didn't need Matthew either – except maybe when he was tied up in a foxhole, and that kind of thing wasn't apt to happen more than once.

When they stepped out of the woods onto Becca's lawn, they moved into another world. Matthew snapped off the light he carried. Moonlight silvered the grass, the paler back sides of the leaves on the poplar trees, the shingle roof of Becca's house, and the concrete walk to the front door.

"I can go by myself," Becca said when Matthew and Steve moved forward into the yard with her.

"But maybe your parents might have some questions," Matthew said, though he stopped as he spoke. Steve stopped gladly beside him. He didn't want to follow Becca to the door and hear her explain to her father about what a liar he was – a big, fat liar.

"I can answer their questions," Becca replied, and she hurried toward the front door, leaving Matthew and Steve standing on the edge of the woods.

They stood waiting until she had disappeared into the brightly lit house, and then they turned toward the path through the alfalfa field.

Matthew walked close beside Steve, but he didn't try to touch him in any way. Still, he kept pace with Steve's steps, and Steve could have wagered that Matthew's breathing matched his own and his heartbeat, too. But of course that was silly. Matthew had been gone for three years, and he had come back practically a stranger. There was hardly anything about him that matched with Steve anymore.

They walked side by side, even along the narrow path through the alfalfa. A small breeze had sprung up, rustling the corn in the field off to the right, lifting the heat a little.

"It's a serious thing," Matthew said finally, "what you and Becca did and what the others did."

Steve nodded.

"You know Donny will probably never have another new bike, not for years anyway."

"Yeah. I know."

"And you and Becca might have been badly hurt when you were knocked into the foxhole . . . or if I hadn't been home, you might not have been found for a long time. I was the only one who knew where to look."

Steve nodded again. They had arrived at the cinder alley that ran behind the houses, and stopped walking to face each other.

"All that time you were sitting in the foxhole, did you figure anything you could do about Donny's bike? There's lots of time for thinking in the quiet of a foxhole."

Huh, Steve thought, *you've never been tied back to back*

with Becca if you think it was quiet, but he only said, "No. I thought a lot. But I couldn't figure anything. I thought of paint remover . . . to take it all off. But I suppose the store paint would come off with what I put on."

"Yes. I suppose it would."

"I couldn't think of anything else."

Matthew put his hand on Steve's shoulder, let it drop, and began to move slowly along the alley in the direction of their house. "Do you still keep your fortune tucked away in Pig, the way you did before I left home?"

Pig was Steve's bank, a blue ceramic pig with orange cheeks. Matthew always teased Steve because he saved practically every penny of his allowance. He was always saving for something, but when it came time to buy the object of his desire, he could rarely bear to part with the money, so he went on saving for something more magnificent. It was hearing the coins clink in Pig's stomach, the sound growing softer and higher as the pile grew, that pleased him most, more than anything he could own.

"Yeah," he said cautiously. "I do." He wondered what Matthew was thinking of. He surely didn't expect him to buy Donny a new bike. At twenty cents a week, it would take him years to get that much money. Besides, he was saving for a new electric train, a passenger train like the new diesel streamliners to hook up next to the old freight train that had been Matthew's once.

"I wonder," Matthew said, "how much it would cost to take Donny's bike into the bike shop and have them give it a professional paint job."

Steve stopped walking and scuffed at the cinders. They

had arrived at their own backyard. "I suppose I would have enough money for that. And Becca might help, even if she is mad at me." He couldn't keep from sighing a little at the thought of Pig's empty belly, but even so, a feeling was growing in his chest, of relief, release. He would tell Donny first thing in the morning.

"Good boy!" Matthew ruffled his hair, and Steve pulled away, but playfully. He raised his fists in a mock boxing stance and danced around Matthew, who laughed and reached out to cuff Steve lightly on the side of the head. But then Matthew was serious again, and Steve stopped the fooling and fell in beside him as they walked through the backyard toward the house.

"Do you think your offer will cool Ray Celestino's little war?" Matthew asked.

Steve shrugged. "I don't know. Celestino doesn't like me. He hasn't liked me since the first day he laid eyes on me."

"What do you say," Matthew asked, stopping at the back steps, "we call a conference of the Big Five tomorrow . . . see if we can find our way to peace."

"Celestino will never listen. The twins might, but Celestino won't."

"Not even if I'm there?"

Steve considered that. Would Celestino listen to Matthew? Probably not. But he wouldn't dare say the things he'd said before to Matthew's face, either. And maybe the twins would hear, would remember that Matthew had been their friend before, too. Maybe Becca would even get over being mad.

Of course Matthew might make things worse – like a teacher trying to settle a fight on the playground by insisting that the contenders shake hands.

"I don't know," he said. A rectangle of warm yellow light streamed through the screen door, and Steve could see the hopeful, almost pleading look in Matthew's face. The whole thing seemed terribly important to him.

Steve made a fist and tapped Matthew lightly in the ribs. "But we can try," he said. "They can't kill us for trying."

CHAPTER 9

Matthew walked up and down on one side of the foxhole as he spoke, his hands clasped behind his back, his face creased in earnestness. Four of the "Big Five" sat or reclined, while Celestino stood, shifting his weight from time to time. Steve sat at one end where he could watch Matthew and the changing expressions on the others' faces as well. In fact, he was having a hard time keeping track of what Matthew was saying, he was so busy trying to guess how the others were reacting to each word.

"So . . . Donny." Matthew looked from one twin's face to the other until Donny identified himself by reacting. "Steve and Becca have an offer to make."

"We'll pay to have your bike repainted – any color you want," Steve said.

"At a bike shop," Becca added, not looking in Steve's direction, "so it'll look good."

"And I'll take it in to the shop and bring it back," Matthew concluded. "Does that sound fair to you?"

Before he answered, Donny looked at Celestino, obviously

waiting for orders. Celestino was whittling a stick with his jackknife and he didn't even glance in Donny's direction.

"I guess so," Donny mumbled, banging his heels against the side of the foxhole. Again he looked over at Celestino, who threw him a dark, scornful glance that made Donny's back slump into an S-curve.

"Will it be as good as new?" Kenny asked. He was on his stomach, plucking long stems of grass, one at a time.

"No." Matthew shook his head. "It will be a lot better than it is now, but it won't look just like a factory paint job, if that's what you mean."

"Yeah," Celestino said, "that's what he means." He moved to the edge of the foxhole and spoke directly to Matthew. "What I want to know is, if it ain't gonna be good as new, why should Donny be satisfied?"

"Because it's the best that can be done," Matthew replied, keeping his voice quiet, his steady eyes taking Celestino's measure. "Some things, once done, can't be undone. Like leaving those two tied in the woods for hours."

"They got out," Celestino said, turning his palms up. Their escape might have been a gift he was offering.

Matthew nodded in agreement. "They got out. Not quite as good as new, however."

Steve glanced over at Becca, who was listening to all of this with solemn interest. Her face was still swollen, though most of the bites had subsided to hard, pink welts. She looked like someone with a case of giant measles, and there were rope burns on her wrists and ankles. Of course, when he had passed a mirror that morning, he had seen that he didn't look much better.

"Them two started the whole thing," Celestino said, a warning in his voice.

"We didn't do anything to them until they took Donny's bike," Kenny pointed out.

Matthew nodded at Kenny. "I know. It's their fault, too. The fault is everybody's, actually. Yours and your brother's and Steve's and Becca's and Ray's."

Steve had almost expected Matthew to stop before he got to Ray Celestino's name, but he looked Celestino straight in the eye and named him along with all the others.

"I don't know how the world can expect to keep the peace," Matthew added, "when a handful of kids can't keep it on their own block."

"Is that what you was doing with the Japs?" Celestino asked. "Keeping the peace?"

Steve could see the muscles in Matthew's jaw working, but he answered calmly. "I was praying for it, I can tell you that. Every time I fired a gun, I prayed for peace."

Celestino's face was perfectly smooth, deceptively pleasant. "Was it peace you was praying for when you led your buddies away from all them Japs?"

Steve swallowed hard. He looked to see how far he would have to go to be able to disappear into the woods. He should have thought of this before, that someone – especially Celestino – would bring up the story he had told about Matthew. He peeked at Matthew out of the corner of his eye. His brother was looking bewildered.

Celestino took a step closer to Matthew. "Or maybe you just forgot. Maybe you done so many brave things that there's some of 'em you can't remember. Your little brother told us all about the smoke screen you threw up in front of them Japs . . . with grenades. You musta got that medal he says you have for lettin' them all live, it being more dangerous that way and all."

A smile pulled at the corners of Matthew's mouth, but he didn't look at Steve. He lowered his head. "I don't have a medal," he said softly. Then he added, "Besides, I was artillery, and artillery aren't issued grenades."

Celestino took another step closer to Matthew, his eyes narrowed to dark slits. "But Steve said – "

"Steve has always had an excellent imagination," Matthew interrupted, and he looked Celestino full in the face as if an "excellent imagination" might be something to boast of.

Kenny and Donny were watching Steve's discomfort with evident satisfaction. Even Becca seemed pleased, as though she had bitten into something that tasted juicy and sweet.

"Then he lied about what you did in the war," Celestino said.

Matthew shrugged, but he still didn't look over at Steve. "I guess he made up some stories, to fill in for my not telling him anything myself. It's understandable enough."

"What did you do, then?" Kenny asked.

"Yeah, what?" Donny seconded.

"I already told you" – Matthew's mouth was tight – "I was artillery."

"You got a Purple Heart?" Celestino asked.

Matthew shook his head. "No. I was one of the lucky ones. I wasn't wounded." And then he added, as if Celestino were some kind of friend, "I know your dad was wounded, and I'm sorry. It's hard on a man to have his work taken away."

Steve had heard that Mr. Celestino once operated big

machinery – steam shovels and Caterpillars like those used in the mill quarry – but of course he couldn't do that with one stiff leg, which was why he was a night watchman now.

Celestino pulled his GI fatigue cap down onto his forehead until the brim hid his eyes. "You don't need to feel sorry for my old man."

Matthew looked to the others, apparently ready to change the subject, but Celestino added, "He don't feel sorry for you. He says you're yellow."

Now Matthew will pound Celestino, Steve thought, but though Matthew's mouth was pinched, he still stood loosely, his muscles relaxed, as if he hadn't heard anything that would make him take offense. "What I'm concerned about," he said, "is you kids . . . the wounds you're inflicting. Do you think there's some way we can call a halt to your war?" He looked at the twins' faces and then at Steve and Becca, avoiding Celestino.

Celestino, who didn't like being ignored, raised his voice. "I think Steve was right. I don't think you ever killed a single Jap."

Matthew's lips went white. "When we were at war," he said, still looking at the other four, not at Celestino, "I fought . . . I killed . . . exactly as I was told to do."

Killed! Steve snapped to attention. Matthew had never killed anyone.

"But when the war was over," Matthew continued, "when the armistice was signed, the army kept me right there, in Japan. And I learned that the people we were fighting were . . . just that. People . . . human beings like us."

"Those dirty yellow monkeys?" Celestino's voice rose with genuine astonishment.

"And I learned" – Matthew increased his volume to speak over anything further Celestino might say – "that even if they did start the war with us, bombing Pearl Harbor, we had done some terrible things . . . in the name of winning the peace . . . and I was . . . I was . . ." Matthew drew himself up, held his breath for a moment until the word came out with explosive power: "ashamed."

The silence that followed Matthew's declaration was louder than any of his words had been. Even the woods sounds had gone still in response. And then Celestino repeated, the question little more than a whisper, "Ashamed?"

"Yes," Matthew answered, on the defensive now. "At least I had the sense to know that shame was called for. That's more than I can say for some who were there."

"There's some who was there," Celestino said, "who wasn't ashamed of nothing. They even got wounded, and they wasn't ashamed of that, either."

You're not ashamed, Steve pleaded silently. *Tell him. You've done nothing to make you that way.*

But Matthew didn't hear, or if he did hear, he didn't care, because he didn't so much as look in Steve's direction. He stood perfectly still for an instant, and then he bowed toward Celestino, actually bowed, a curious, old-fashioned gesture such as a butler in a movie might make before leaving a room. Then he nodded to the others, his lips pressed tightly together and the skin around his nose gray-white, pivoted on one foot, and strode out of the clearing without a word or a backward glance.

A collective sigh passed through the group like a faint wind moving through trees, and Kenny giggled once in a high-pitched rush, like a girl. Steve watched them all through blurred eyes, his friends. At least they had been his friends once . . . except for Celestino. Now Matthew had spoiled everything.

He swallowed hard. "Don't listen to him," he said. "Don't listen to anything he says. He doesn't know what he's talking about."

Nobody answered. They stared at Steve, and he had to go on talking or be shut away from them forever. "Matthew's always made up stories. That's what he did when I was a little kid . . . all the time. He didn't mean what he said . . . about killing people . . . about being ashamed. He didn't mean any of it."

"It was a war," Donny said, as if he was explaining something Steve didn't understand.

"Well, Matthew didn't kill anybody," Steve shouted. "Not once!"

"He had to." It was Becca, know-it-all Becca. "He didn't have any choice."

"He was a soldier," Kenny added.

"They couldn't make him," Steve said, tugging on the front of his shirt, licking his lips. "He had his ways. They couldn't make him kill anybody."

"What ways?" It was Celestino moving in closer, towering over Steve.

Steve looked away from Celestino, across the clearing in the direction that Matthew had taken. Maybe he hadn't gone away. Maybe he was still waiting there, just inside the screen of trees. He might come back to help.

"What ways did your big brother have?" Celestino demanded. He was still holding the open jackknife in his hand.

Kenny chimed in. "Matthew was a gunner, and a gunner kills people. Lots of them. Those big guns could kill a whole mess of Japs at one time. Ka-pow! Boom!" And Kenny spread his hands as wide as they would go, demonstrating the extent of the destruction a howitzer could accomplish.

Steve rubbed his nose with the back of his hand. Why had Matthew gone off and left him here to explain? Steve didn't know any answers. He only knew what he had known the whole time Matthew was gone. His brother couldn't hurt anybody – not even Japs. He wasn't made for killing. That was all.

"What ways?" Celestino repeated, taking another step closer, the blade of the knife glinting where it extended from his hand.

"Matthew was the one who aimed the howitzer," Steve said. The words stumbled from his mouth without his bidding. "I mean, he made the adjustments to figure where it would fire."

"Yeah?" Celestino was standing so close that Steve could smell his sweat.

"And he always used to figure the adjustments so the gun would fire short – or to one side – or long. Just so it wouldn't hit anybody. Nobody ever knew. None of the other guys in his platoon ever figured out what he was doing."

Becca had gone pale. Donny and Kenny stared, first at one another and then at Steve. Their mouths formed matching O's.

"Well, now," Celestino said, and he was smiling. "That's real interesting. How did you find out about it?"

Steve searched through the dull ache that had taken residence where his brain was supposed to be. How did he know . . . about adjusting the big gun? He couldn't remember. "Matthew told me," he said.

Celestino's teeth were showing. They were very white. "Seems strange he would tell something like that . . . even to his little brother."

Steve glanced over at Becca, who was staring at him in a way that hurt his skin. "He got drunk one night," he said quickly, looking away from Becca. "He had too much beer and he told me all kinds of things. He probably doesn't even remember telling me," he added, "but he never killed anybody."

Celestino threw away the stick he had been whittling on, snapped his jackknife closed, and pocketed it. "Then it's true, what my old man said." He nodded with satisfaction.

"What was that?" Kenny asked. "What did your old man say?"

"He said" – Celestino turned to talk to the twins, as though what he said had nothing to do with Steve – "that Steve's big brother is a Jap-lover."

Steve's stomach lurched. "That's not true!" he cried.

Celestino turned slowly to face him. "But he adjusted that big gun so it wouldn't hit nobody. You said so. If that ain't being a Jap-lover, I don't know what is."

"The more Japs lived," Donny said solemnly, "the more American soldiers died."

Steve opened his mouth to speak, but nothing came out. After a few seconds he closed it again. Everybody was looking at him, waiting for what he would say, all four of them, lined up against him . . . against him and Matthew.

"Matthew's no Jap-lover," he said. He turned mechanically, walked a few steps and then turned back. "And he's got nothing to be ashamed of at all."

The four faces kept watching him without the slightest change in expression.

CHAPTER 10

Steve hugged his chest as he walked down the red slag street, trying to hold the anger close. It was Matthew's fault . . . the whole thing. Sometimes Matthew didn't have the sense that God gave chickens.

To say such a thing – in front of everybody!

Steve still didn't know if he had been defending Matthew or damning him. The kids had thought what he said about Matthew was terrible, but he didn't mean for it to be . . . did he?

Matthew had killed. He said he had. And that didn't even seem to be the reason he was ashamed.

Steve flung open the screen door and let it slam behind him. It didn't make a loud enough noise. He wanted to turn around and slam it again. His mother was in the kitchen, ironing a shirt . . . probably one of Matthew's. Her face was rosy from the combined heat of the afternoon and the iron.

"Hi, sweetie. Home in plenty of time for supper for a change." Her voice had a throaty, musical quality that made it impossible for Steve to resent baby endearments like "sweetie." Still, he hunched his shoulders and didn't reply.

He lifted the lid off a pan on the stove, and grease popped at him like stinging bullets. He let the lid clatter back into place and rubbed the spots on his arm where the hot grease had spattered him. "What's for supper?"

"Matthew's favorite." His mother smiled.

Of course, what else? He lifted the lid again, cautiously. "What's that supposed to be?" Matthew's favorite looked like an assortment of small gray mice.

"Chicken livers sautéed in butter. Don't you remember what Matthew likes?"

Steve let the lid settle back onto the pan again, scarcely more quietly than he had dropped it the first time. "You can give my share to Ginger," he said, and he headed through the living room to the front door. "She can have Matthew's, too, for all I care." He shoved the screen door as he went through it so it would slam harder this time. It was one of his mother's pet peeves, slamming doors.

"Steve!" she called, but he rammed his hands into his pockets and lumbered down the front steps, pretending he hadn't heard.

Why had he told that terrible story about Matthew? It wasn't true, not any part of it. It wasn't any more true than the story about the grenades.

"An excellent imagination." That's what Matthew had called it, but the kids said Steve was a liar.

And he was.

He was worse than a liar.

He remembered now where the story had come from, about Matthew adjusting the big gun so it wouldn't hit anybody. It was the one he had told himself all the time

Matthew was fighting the war, because he couldn't stand the idea of his big brother killing anybody. Not even Japs. He hadn't told it to anyone else, of course, but he had repeated it to himself nearly every day.

He had known he wasn't being a loyal American to think that way. Japs were the enemy. Japs and Nazis and Fascists. You were supposed to be glad to have them killed.

But not by his own brother, the one who had given him piggyback rides and come in and sat by his bed when the night was dark and Mom and Dad were too far away.

Steve's being a liar was probably Matthew's fault, anyway . . . all those stories Matthew used to tell. When Steve was a little kid, Matthew was always filling him with stories . . . lies. So what did he expect, anyway?

Maybe Steve's story, the one he had just told, was Matthew's fault, too. Maybe having a big brother who was ashamed of his country, ashamed of being a soldier, rubbed off, even when that big brother was a long way away.

Matthew had killed. He said so himself.

Steve sat down on the curb, picked up a stick, and began drawing patterns in the red slag. He drew an explosion – arms and legs flying from a central core of fire. That's what happened when you shot people with a big gun.

Steve had been sitting on the curb for a long time when he saw them coming, Celestino and the twins. Becca wasn't with them anymore. Steve wasn't surprised at that. She and Kenny had probably gotten into a fight.

"Hey, Pulaski," Celestino called.

Steve bent over his picture and didn't answer. He erased

everything, rubbing it out with one foot and started again, leaning over, intent.

"Whatcha doing?" Kenny sat down on one side of Steve, Donny on the other. Celestino stood in the street, his scuffed, leather shoes covering the top of Steve's new drawing.

"Move, will you?" Steve poked at the toe of Celestino's shoe with the stick, half-expecting Celestino to wallop him. To his surprise, Celestino backed up a few inches. Steve returned to his drawing. He was drawing stick figures, three of them. No, four. He added one with a skirt, then crossed it out, then crossed them all out.

"We got a plan, Pulaski," Celestino said, "and if you ain't a Jap-lover like your brother, we'll let you in."

Steve lifted his eyes to Celestino's face. "I'm no Jap-lover," he said.

Donny was a little breathless. "We told Celestino that."

"But we have to have proof," Kenny reminded his brother.

"What are you talking about?" Steve looked from one twin to the other. They were equally solemn.

"We've written a letter," Kenny explained.

"To J. Edgar Hoover," Donny added.

Avoiding looking at Celestino, who was still directly in front of him, Steve asked, "The head G-man? What do you want to write him for?" The skin was beginning to prickle on the back of his neck.

"Because he's in charge of the FBI," Kenny said, as if that explained anything. "He's the most important man in the whole country."

"After President Truman," Donny contributed.

"He's more important than President Truman, because

Truman hasn't got a chance to get elected again – Dad says – and Mr. Hoover doesn't have to get elected. He's always going to be head G-man."

"While he lives in the White House, the president's still more important," Donny insisted.

"Why are you writing J. Edgar Hoover?" Steve demanded loudly, and the twins fell silent. They looked to Celestino for a reply.

Celestino spoke smoothly, confidentially, as if he shared a special secret with Steve alone. "We're doing something for Uncle Sam that's gonna make us heroes."

"Like what?" Steve couldn't imagine anything that could turn Celestino into a hero.

"We're reporting your big brother to the FBI."

The prickling had moved into Steve's scalp. "What are you talking about? You've got nothing on Matthew to report him for."

"You heard him," Kenny said. He stood up next to Celestino. "You heard what he said . . . about being ashamed." Kenny seemed to be balancing between excitement and apprehension.

"So?" Steve gripped his drawing stick more tightly. "That's nothing. This is a free country."

"Loose lips sink ships," Donny quoted from the poster that used to hang in the post office.

"But we're not fighting anymore," Steve explained, his voice steady, reasonable. "Nobody's sinking ships."

"And of course," Celestino continued, "there's the little story Matthew told you when he was drunk . . . about aiming the gun."

Steve stood up slowly. His knees felt loose, unreliable.

"Can I see it?" he asked. "The letter you've written."

Celestino took a sheet of yellow tablet paper out of his back pocket. "That's what we come over for. Here, Riley." Celestino handed the paper to Donny. "You read it to him."

"Don't let him get his hands on it," Kenny warned. "We don't know yet if he's loyal."

Donny took the piece of paper, unfolded it carefully, cleared his throat as though he were going to read in front of class, and began.

> *Dear Mr. J. Edgar Hoover,*
>
> We are writing to you to report something important. It is about our neighbor, Matthew Pulaski. He is a veteran, but he is not a loyal American. He talks about the United States doing terrible things to win the war. He says he's ashamed. And he ought to be, really. Only it's himself he ought to be ashamed of. When he was in the army, he was a gunner. He was in charge of aiming a howitzer. Only he always made sure it was aimed to not hit any Japs. We know, because once he drunk too much beer and told his brother, Steve, and Steve told us. We all think that Matthew Pulaski should be punished. Because we can't have a good country if everybody doesn't believe.
>
> Yours loyally,
Raymond Celestino
Kenneth Riley
Donald Riley

Donny looked up cautiously when he was finished reading. He looked first at his brother, then at Celestino, and finally he looked at Steve.

"I wrote the letter," he said, and his voice, though prideful, came out small. "The others helped, but mostly I wrote it."

"And you're going to mail it?" Steve's question rose to a thin squeak at the end.

"Sure." Celestino took the piece of paper back from Donny, folded it carefully along the fold lines, slipped it into his back pocket. "You don't think we want a traitor running loose in our neighborhood, do you?"

"He ought to get quite a few years in the slammer after J. Edgar Hoover reads that," Kenny said.

"But it's not true," Steve blurted.

The eyebrow of Celestino's that seemed to operate independently of the rest of his face went up. "Of course it's true. We heard him say it ourselves . . . about being ashamed."

"I mean the rest of it . . . about aiming the gun so he wouldn't kill any Japs. That's not true."

Celestino's mouth turned down into an exaggerated frown. "But you told us, just a little bit ago, you told us the whole thing."

Steve opened and closed his mouth several times before the words came out. "I lied. I made it all up . . . everything I said."

Celestino looked from Donny to Kenny. "Do you believe that, men?"

The two boys shook their heads in unison.

Celestino shook his head as well. "I don't believe it either. Nobody would make up a story like that about his own brother."

"They would, too!" Steve was practically shouting. "I mean, I would. You know I tell stories. You've heard me before. I didn't mean to. It just came out." Steve looked from one boy to the other, pleading. "Don't mail the letter," he asked softly.

"Don't mail the letter!" Celestino threw his head back and laughed. "Do you think we spent all that time writing it and now we're going to throw it away?"

"Please." Steve looked up at Celestino. He was begging. He would have gone down on his knees if he had thought it would do any good.

"And here we came to see if you wanted to be a hero, too." Kenny was grinning, obviously enjoying himself.

"What do you mean?"

"We were going to let you sign the letter," Kenny explained. "Then nobody could figure you for a Jap-lover."

"Sign the letter? Against Matthew?"

"You told the story against him, didn't you?" Donny asked.

"But that was – " Steve stopped.

"Different?" Celestino inquired. "That what you was going to say?"

Steve didn't know any longer what he had been going to say. Everything was whirling inside his brain. Matthew would probably go to prison. That's what the FBI did, didn't it? – hauled people off to prison.

And it was all Steve's fault.

"I'll buy the letter from you," he said.

"Buy it!" Celestino scoffed. "You ain't got enough money to buy the first line."

"I'll give you all the money I've got saved up in Pig."

"You mean the money you were gonna use to repaint my bike?" Donny asked innocently.

"I mean all that's left . . . after the bike's painted." Steve was desperate. He had never been so desperate in all his life.

Celestino shook his head. "We're loyal citizens, Pulaski. You can't bribe us."

"I'm not trying to bribe you, I'm just – " Steve stopped again, bit his lip. He couldn't go any further.

"What are you just?" Donny asked. He asked it like he really wanted to know.

"I'm a liar," Steve blurted out. "I'm a big, fat liar." And he turned and ran into the house, swinging the wooden door shut behind himself with a resounding slam.

CHAPTER 11

Matthew was the one who didn't show up for dinner that night. *Maybe the FBI's already come*, Steve worried, but then he reminded himself that was silly. The mailman didn't pick up the mail until morning.

Would a man as important as J. Edgar Hoover believe a letter from a bunch of kids? Steve sat and pushed the chicken livers around on his plate, trying to decide. He hid one beneath a curl of lettuce, disguised another in the middle of his beets, hoping it looked as though he had eaten some. But he didn't know what J. Edgar Hoover would do.

Surely the FBI would know that the story about aiming the howitzer wasn't true. There would have been other soldiers there. They would know. And as for Matthew's being ashamed, they didn't arrest people for that, did they?

"What's the matter, dear?" his mother asked. "Aren't you hungry?"

"Becca and I had onion-top sandwiches in the garden just a little while ago," he explained, trying to smile in his mother's direction. It was a lie, of course, but what was one more lie on a day like today? He and Becca often did take buttered bread to the garden and cut the tops of onions to make sandwiches.

There was only one thing to be done. He would have to get the letter back. It shouldn't be too hard. Everybody put their mail out in their mailboxes right by the front door for the mailman to get early in the morning. All he had to do was to wait until after dark and check the twins' and Celestino's mailboxes.

It was a federal crime to tamper with the mail. His father had told him that once. But if his parents had to choose between his going to jail or Matthew's, they would probably choose for him to go, wouldn't they? At least they would if they knew what he'd done.

"I think I'll go upstairs and read for a while," he said as he rose from the table. And then, in response to his parents' surprised looks, he added, "Everybody's busy tonight. Nobody's going to be out after supper playing."

He wondered as he climbed the stairs if lying was like a disease that took hold of a person, rotting the brain and the tongue until they were incapable of telling the truth.

Steve closed his door behind himself, flipped on the light against the dusky silence of his room, and stood blinking at the figure sprawled the entire length of his bed. It was Matthew.

"Hi," Steve said, his voice changing pitch three times in the single word.

Matthew didn't answer. He just sat up slowly, swung his feet off the bed, ran his wide fingers through his hair.

"You missed supper," Steve said. "Mom had chicken livers . . . special for you." Steve hadn't planned to say that. The words popped out of his mouth – as usual.

Matthew wrinkled his nose, smiled apologetically. "I must have liked chicken livers once. Mom tells me I did."

"You mean you don't like them anymore?"

Matthew shrugged, sighed. "I guess a lot of things changed when I was over there . . . about me, I mean."

"Yeah," Steve said, trying to rescue a scrap of his former anger, "like you got ashamed of your country."

"Not of my country, Steve. Just of some of the things we did."

"What's the difference?"

"Lots. I love my country. I would defend it again if it were necessary. I hope it won't be necessary, though . . . for me or for you."

Steve stood leaning against the door, waiting to see why Matthew was there, what he wanted. Did he know about Steve's story, about the letter? Maybe he had stayed close by in the woods, as Steve had hoped. Maybe he had heard. A trickle of sweat ran down the side of Steve's face, and he swiped at it impatiently.

"I just wanted to tell you I'm sorry," Matthew said. He was tugging at the tufts of Steve's chenille bedspread, not looking at Steve.

"What's there to be sorry for?"

"For making a fool of myself in front of your friends. For going off and leaving you to defend me the way I did."

Leaving you to defend me. Steve's legs felt weak. What would he say if he knew how Steve had defended him? Steve walked across the room and sat down on the bed, a careful distance from Matthew so he wouldn't have to see his face. "It's all right," he said. "They aren't really my friends anyway."

Matthew didn't say anything more, and Steve picked up his pillow and hugged it to his chest the way he used to do when he was a little boy and needed comforting.

"Were they pretty rough on you after I left?" Matthew asked gently.

Steve straightened his back, laid the pillow down again and patted it smooth. *No more stories*, he told himself sternly. *If you tell Matthew, he can help you get the letter back. Maybe he'll tell you a letter from a bunch of kids is nothing to worry about.* But when he opened his mouth, the lie simply tumbled out. "I took care of them, all right. I told them that you had a right to feel any way you wanted to, that you'd killed as many Japs as anybody and you had a right."

"Oh, Steve," Matthew breathed. "You don't understand, do you? You don't understand any part of it."

Steve looked at Matthew in astonishment. "What don't I understand?"

"What I was talking about."

The heat rose to Steve's face. "How do you expect me to understand?"

Matthew shrugged. He was tugging on the bedspread again.

"You don't talk to me anymore," Steve said, keeping his voice low but the words coming out rapidly. "You don't tell me anything. You used to talk to me all the time, even when I was only a little kid and must have been dull as dirt. Now you don't say two words from morning to night."

Instead of arguing, Matthew nodded his head. "You're right," he said. "You're absolutely right."

And then they sat like that, side by side, saying nothing.

You fink, Steve accused himself in the silence. *You lied again. You didn't defend Matthew. You made everything worse.* But out loud he said, "I'm not too much of a kid to understand if you'd explain things."

Matthew shook his head, and at first Steve thought he still wasn't going to tell him anything, but then he said, "You heard about it back here. I know you did. But nobody knows what it was like."

"What?" Steve demanded, almost roughly. "What was it we heard about?"

Matthew buried his face in his hands, and his voice was muffled. "The bomb."

"The what?"

Matthew raised his head so that his words came out clearly. "The bomb. The atomic bomb. Two of them, really. We dropped one on Hiroshima and one on Nagasaki. You knew about that, surely?"

Steve nodded. He knew. Those were the bombs that had ended the war in the Pacific. People had rejoiced when they had discovered that their country had such a weapon – to end wars.

"Do you know what those bombs did?"

Steve nodded again. Of course. Everybody knew.

"The city of Hiroshima," Matthew said, going right on as if Steve had asked him to. "I saw it . . . afterward . . . and I talked to some of the people, some who could speak English. The whole city was blown over . . . collapsed . . . like a town made out of matchsticks. And the people . . ." He choked, shook his head, clearing away the sound of tears. "I saw the people. It was like they'd been through a rain of fire."

Matthew's hands rested on his knees. The fine, red-gold hairs on the backs shone in the light from the overhead bulb. "A rain of fire?" Steve repeated, leaning back against the head of the bed and studying Matthew's face.

Matthew straightened his back, tipped his chin up, like an animal listening. Steve tried to listen, too, but there was nothing to hear.

"It was morning," Matthew said, "early. Children were finishing breakfast or on their way to school, playing along the way as children do. There was a plane. One lone plane. They saw it, most of them, but they didn't worry. Who would send one plane alone to fight a war?" He stopped, waited, still listening, but then he didn't go on.

"And that was when we did it?" Steve asked finally, wanting him to finish, wanting him to come to the end so he would stop.

"That was when we did it," Matthew repeated, like a slow child repeating a lesson. "We dropped the first atomic bomb."

"But we had to, Matthew. Didn't we? Thousands would have been killed if we hadn't . . . our own soldiers. *You*, maybe."

Matthew's back stiffened. "I never asked them to save my life," he burst out. "Not like that!"

Steve clamped his mouth shut. It wasn't possible to say anything right.

"It was terrible," Matthew whispered. "People trapped beneath buildings. People running in the streets, the burned and blackened flesh hanging from their bones in long strips. 'Water!' they kept crying. 'Water!' Everybody talked about that – the way they cried for water. And they threw themselves, dying, into the river until the river was filled from bank to bank with bodies."

Steve shuddered. He wanted to block his ears.

"And after it was over," Matthew said, turning slowly to face Steve for the first time, "the radiation sickness began. That's the way they were when I saw them, lots of the ones who were left . . . dying by inches, and none of us, not even the doctors, knew anything to do for them. Not anything at all."

Steve tried to retreat from his brother's stare, but there was no place to go.

Matthew stood up, his eyes keeping their hold. "There was a little boy there . . . in the hospital where I visited. He was just your age . . . or he was the age you'd been when I'd seen you last. And he reminded me of you."

"Was he – " Steve started to say, but Matthew ignored his question and went on.

"Oh, his hair was a different color and his eyes were a different shape, and the bones made a little different pattern in his face" – Matthew brushed away the differences with the back of his hand – "but when he grinned or teased . . . or cried, he was exactly like you."

"But he was a Jap, wasn't he?"

For an instant Matthew looked surprised, perhaps angry, but then he shook his head and replied evenly, "No. He was a boy, Steve. Just a Japanese boy. His name was Seiji."

"Saygee?"

"It means Star Child."

"What happened to him?"

"He died. Seiji was the last of his family to go. He had no one left to sit with him the last three days except me, and I think he was afraid of me." Matthew released Steve from his gaze then, withdrew his probing stare, and sat examining his big hands as if he could see there traces of the bomb that had done such terrible things to Seiji, to his family.

Steve wanted to reach out to take one of those hands, but instead he said, gently, as if explaining something to a child, "But you didn't drop the bomb. It wasn't you."

Matthew shook his head slowly from side to side. "It was all of us, Steve. Me . . . you. It was our children who haven't been born. Either we take responsibility or nobody ever will." For an instant Matthew's eyes met Steve's squarely, eyes filled with pleading. Steve felt included, drawn into the circle of his brother's pain. But then Matthew sighed, stood up.

"Never mind," he said. "I know you don't understand. How could I expect you to? Nobody else does. Not even Dad." He started for the door.

Steve was stunned. He had been tossed away as easily as he had been gathered in. Watching the retreating curve of his brother's back, Steve felt the weight of Matthew's burden settling onto his own shoulders. What right did Matthew have to carry such stories home, such terrible stories that no one else knew, or would want to hear?

When Matthew had one hand on the doorknob, he spoke again. "It's not much of a world we leave you, little brother, protected by atomic bombs."

"Maybe it *was* your fault," Steve spat out, before Matthew could make his escape from the room, "the bomb and all the people it killed, but it's not mine. Nothing any of you did over there was any fault of mine."

Matthew's face twisted, but his voice remained calm. "You're probably right," he said, nodding his head like a simpleton, and that made Steve angrier still.

"It's probably all a lie, anyway, another one of your lies." Steve's eyes met Matthew's gaze and then slid away to a corner of the room. "All my life that's all you've done . . . told me lies."

If Steve had slapped Matthew, if he had punched him in the belly or stomped on his bare foot, Matthew couldn't have looked more hurt. But he stood in Steve's doorway, perfectly erect, saying nothing to defend himself. It was as bad as it had been when Matthew had faced Celestino's derision . . . worse.

Steve wanted him to strike back . . . with words, with his fists, but Matthew merely nodded and closed the door quietly between them.

Steve sat on the edge of his bed for a long time, keeping his mind carefully, mercifully blank. Finally he lay down and covered his head with the pillow, not bothering to get up to turn off the staring overhead light.

CHAPTER 12

Steve pushed the pillow away and sat up in bed. Had he slept? He checked out the Big Ben alarm clock on his dresser. Eleven-fifteen. His window was completely black. He must have slept . . . and dreamed.

Was it a dream, the children running, the charred bodies filling the river? The boy named Star Child who died while Matthew watched?

Why had Matthew stayed to watch? You could bet the other soldiers weren't sitting around hospitals with dying kids. He had said Seiji reminded him of Steve. Then maybe it was all Steve's fault, Matthew's sitting there in the hospital and getting strange.

Steve stood up and tiptoed to the hall, down the stairs, out the front door, closing the screen door quietly behind him. On the porch he hesitated. What was he going to do? Then he remembered the letter. That was it. He was going to get the letter.

He wasn't sure why he cared what happened to Matthew. Maybe he didn't, really. Maybe he just didn't want any part of it to be his fault.

Celestino and the twins would never know the postman hadn't picked the letter up early in the morning. And the whole thing would be forgotten in a little while – including Steve's story.

He couldn't imagine now why he had ever told himself a story like that. Of course Matthew had fought. And the big gun he aimed had killed people . . . Japs . . . Japanese.

Maybe Matthew had killed Seiji's father or older brother. But a gun was better than an atomic bomb. Wasn't it? Well, wasn't it?

Steve didn't know. He didn't understand anything anymore except that he had to get the letter back. He had to get it back, and he wasn't ever going to tell another lie as long as he lived. He would stop the words from coming if he had to staple his tongue to his lower lip to keep himself still.

He checked the twins' house first. It was easy to walk up onto their front porch. But the letter wasn't there. He hadn't really thought it would be. Celestino would want to be the one to send the letter off.

He moved down off their front porch, through the puddle of light beneath the street lamp, across the street and over to Celestino's side yard. There were still lights on in Celestino's house. He sat down beside a large bush to wait until everyone had gone to bed. He wasn't really afraid of going up onto Celestino's porch, he was just . . . terrified. He might as well admit it to himself. Lying was lying, even when you were your only audience. If Celestino caught him, he would never have another chance at the letter. If he didn't get the letter, Matthew would go to prison.

A half-moon gave out a dim light. The stars seemed almost as close as the fireflies that blinked on and off across the lawn. Steve could tell where the smoke from the cement mill passed directly above, because there was one long strip of sky not clustered with stars.

Something rustled deep inside the bush, and Steve froze. Then there was silence. Just as he was beginning to relax, the sound came again, accompanied by a trilling mew. Ginger!

Steve let out the breath he had been holding. "Do you have to follow me everywhere I go?" he asked the small shadow that purred and rubbed against his side. Maybe if he ignored her she would go away.

He could hear a murmur of sound coming from the house, but he couldn't see anyone. Probably Mr. Celestino was getting ready to go to work. The night watchman's job would start with the twelve o'clock shift.

Ginger stood on her hind legs, her front paws in Steve's lap, and nudged his chin with her cool nose. Steve stroked her absent-mindedly, and she gave his chin a quick, darting lick with her rough tongue. She was such a funny old cat. His mother had gotten her before Steve was born, so he had never known a time when Ginger wasn't around.

The volume of sound from the house had increased, but Steve couldn't make out any of the words. They were probably speaking Italian. Shouting Italian was more like it. Many of the families in the neighborhood spoke a language other than English at home.

There was a sharp cracking sound, repeated several times, and total silence after each of the awful cracks. Was someone being hit? Steve scooted backward, burrowing deeper under the bush. He picked up Ginger and buried his face in her soft, warm fur. Maybe Mr. Celestino beat his wife. Steve had heard of such things, but it was difficult to imagine its actually happening.

A flood of words again, Mrs. Celestino's voice rising higher and higher, Mr. Celestino answering in an angry rumble. There was a crash, like something falling over, and then silence again.

The door burst open. Mr. Celestino was silhouetted against the inside light. He stood – staggered rather – in the doorway for a moment, then moved across the porch and down the steps, swinging his stiff leg ahead, then throwing his weight on it with an angry intensity. At the bottom of the steps he reached out to each side as if to grab the air and steady himself. He was clearly drunk. Steve had never seen anyone in his own family drunk, despite what he had told the kids, but he had seen men lurching out of the taverns that lined the main street of town, so he recognized the symptoms.

Mr. Celestino was going to work, and he was drunk. Maybe that would be useful to know for some time in the future. Mr. Hansen, Becca's father, would hardly want to keep on a drunken night watchman.

Steve crouched deeper into the shadow of the bushes while Mr. Celestino made his way down the street to the path through the field. After he was completely out of sight, the lights in the house began to flick off one by one. The front door opened once, but Steve couldn't see anyone come out onto the shadowed porch. It was probably just Mrs. Celestino checking to see if her husband had made it down the steps, relieved to know he was gone for the night.

Steve waited another several minutes. The porch was dark, covered by a low roof, surrounded by a banistered railing. The mailbox would be right next to the front door. It would be simple to check it, get the letter if it was there, as simple as it had been to walk up onto the twins' porch. Well, almost as simple as that.

"Go home, Ginger," Steve whispered, and he pushed the old cat away. She walked a few steps, her tail twitching in annoyance, then she sat down and licked the middle of her back, washing away the indignity of Steve's push.

Steve crept toward the front porch, keeping low, though there was nothing to hide from now. When he got to the side, below the banistered railing, he hesitated, listening. All was still. He climbed up to the porch, crawled over the railing, and let himself down to the porch floor. The mailbox formed a darker shadow right next to the door. He made for it, and when he reached in, his hand found a letter immediately. He held it up to the faint light from the street, squinting at the address. In an uneven hand was printed J. EDGAR HUVER. How easy this was! He held the letter to his chest, backing toward the porch banister and home.

When Celestino stood up from the other side of the porch, Steve first wondered why he hadn't seen him earlier. Then he realized that the boy had been sitting, stretched out on the hanging porch swing, blending into the dark shape of the swing.

"I thought you'd try something, Pulaski," was all he said.

Steve's first inclination was to run. He had at least half the distance of the porch between them. He could be over the railing and gone, practically before Celestino had a chance to move. But something kept his feet glued to the porch floor, probably the certainty that Celestino would catch up with him wherever he ran.

Celestino took a step toward Steve, then another, then another. "What do you mean, sneaking around my house . . . spying?" And in a single swift movement, like a snake striking, he had the letter out of Steve's hand.

"I told you," Steve said helplessly, "I made that whole story up . . . about the big gun."

Celestino snickered. "Of course you did. I knew you was lying all along."

Steve was dumbfounded. "Then why did you write the letter? Why are you telling those things to Mr. Hoover if you know they aren't true?"

"For the same reason you told them. Because I think Matthew deserves whatever he gets."

"That's not why I made up that story!"

Celestino turned the white envelope over and over in his hands. "Then what was your reason? Did you think you was doing your big brother some kind of favor?"

"No." Steve shook his head. "Because I didn't understand." He was backing up as he spoke.

"You didn't understand, huh? I think you understood plenty."

The banister caught Steve in the middle of the back, stopping his flight. But somehow the feeling of the wooden railing behind him, the solidness of it, gave him courage, and he said, "No, I didn't. Because Matthew hadn't talked to me at all . . . about the war, I mean. About the bomb. About people dying by inches."

Celestino snorted. "I thought people always died by feet. One foot in the grave, you know."

But Steve's words kept tumbling out, as if Celestino weren't trying to turn the whole thing into a joke, as if the older boy could be expected to hear. "He told me about a little boy who reminded him of me. I mean, me at the age I was when he'd seen me last. The boy's name was Star Child. He died . . . while Matthew watched." Celestino didn't say anything more, so Steve continued. "He was the last one in his family to die, so he was all alone. Except for Matthew."

Steve's words seemed to run out like an automobile running out of fuel. He waited.

"Jap-lovers!" Celestino spit it out. "The whole bunch of you, Jap-lovers."

"No, that's not – "

"Your big brother tried to feed my old man that crap – about how we should feel so bad . . . about the bomb . . . about the little children. My old man told him a thing or two about them Japs. He was in a prisoner-of-war camp. That's where he got his bad leg. One of them slant-eyes jabbed him in the leg with a bayonet, for no reason. And then it festered. He almost had to have it cut off. If the war hadn't ended when it did, my pa probably would have died."

So Celestino lied, too, Steve thought, but the realization gave him no satisfaction. "It's not Matthew's fault your father was hurt," he pleaded.

Celestino turned away, just turned around completely so his back was toward Steve.

"Please don't mail that letter."

"Ha!" Celestino laughed, a sharp, humorless explosion. "Why don't you try to stop me?"

Steve didn't move away from the railing. He felt a pressure around his ankles and, without looking down, knew that Ginger had followed him here, too. Just what he needed, his mother's cat for protection. "Maybe I should tell Mr. Hansen that your father goes to work drunk," he said quietly.

Celestino whirled and strode back across the porch. In fact, he moved in so close that Steve could feel the warmth of the taller boy's breath on his forehead. Celestino grabbed the front of Steve's shirt and twisted it, drawing the shirt tight. The twisted fabric cut sharply into Steve's armpits, and the lift of Celestino's hand raised him onto his toes.

"You won't tell Mr. Hansen nothin'. Not if you wanna live."

"Okay," Steve agreed quickly, bobbing his head up and down. "I won't tell Mr. Hansen nothing . . . I mean anything. I really won't," he added as Celestino bounced him off the railing and dropped him to his hands and knees. Ginger was right there, and she rubbed against Steve's face, purring loudly. She seemed to think he had gotten down like that just to play with her.

"Look what we've got here," Celestino said, bending down and scooping Ginger into his hands, pulling her away from Steve's face. "Your mama's cat."

Steve struggled to his feet, a new uneasiness traveling his spine. "You put her down," he warned.

Ginger flexed her claws and purred in Celestino's arms.

"I will," Celestino replied, cupping his hand over her face and running it over the top of her head, forcing her ears back. Then he ran it down the rest of her body so she seemed to emerge from his hand like something squeezed out of a tube. "When I'm good and ready."

"Come on, Celestino," Steve said urgently, and when Celestino kept his hold on Ginger, he added, "What good is that old cat . . . to you, I mean?"

Celestino scratched the patch of white fur on Ginger's throat. She lifted her delicate, V-shaped chin, turning her head this way and that to direct the scratching to her favorite spots, quite oblivious of any threat.

"I want her for a hostage," Celestino explained, his tone reasonable. "Just to make sure you don't go squealing to your girlfriend's papa."

"Me?" Steve asked, and his voice rose to a squeak on the question he created out of the word. He tried to force a laugh, but nothing would come out. "I never even see Becca's father. I was only kidding. I thought you knew that."

Celestino grinned, and for a fraction of a second, Steve thought that approach had worked. "I think," Celestino said, "you just might find a way to see him, if you wanted to bad enough."

"How long are you gonna keep Ginger?" Steve asked, probing for a new approach. "You can't keep her forever."

"Can't I?" Celestino feigned surprise, as if the thought of not being able to keep Steve's mother's cat forever had never occurred to him.

"I promise," Steve said. "I give you my word. I won't tell

Mr. Hansen anything about your dad. I won't tell anybody else either."

"Your word!" Celestino exploded into laughter, and Ginger, startled, began to squirm, trying to free herself. Celestino held her more tightly. "You know what you word is worth?"

Steve didn't answer. He knew. The two stood that way, facing one another. Finally Steve asked, "What, then? What can I do to get her back?"

Celestino seemed to concentrate on petting Ginger for a few moments until she grew calm again. Finally, he spoke. "I tell you what, Pulaski. I've been wantin' to get my hands on some dynamite ever since I come to this place. You slip into the quarry and steal some for me, and I'll give you back your mama's kittycat."

"What do you want with dynamite?" Steve asked.

"Just to fix me up with some more foxholes. That's all. And if you steal it for me, then I'll know you won't do no squealing . . . about nothing, because if you do . . ." Celestino let his words trail off.

Steve's mouth had gone dry. Steal? Dynamite? "What about the letter," he asked. "If I bring you some dynamite, will you give me back the letter?"

Celestino shifted Ginger in his arms. She was purring loudly. He looked down at the envelope in his hand and up at Steve. "You'd better bring me a whole bunch of dynamite. That's all I got to say. A whole bunch."

"But if I bring it," Steve persisted, "a whole bunch, then you'll give me back Ginger and the letter, too?"

Celestino seemed to consider as he stood there. He held the letter up, and Ginger reached to pat it with one white-tipped paw. The envelope and the white fur of the paw reflected the street lamp and seemed to throw a near-light onto Celestino's face. "The cat," he said, "I guarantee. I've got no use for your mama's cat. The letter" – he held it higher, turned it over as if to examine the other side – "well, we'll see about that when I get a look at what you bring."

CHAPTER 13

Steve sat at the kitchen table, stirring his soggy corn flakes, pressing them down to the bottom of the bowl with the back of his spoon and watching them rise to the surface of the milk again.

His mother repeated her question. "Has either of you seen Ginger?"

"What's wrong?" his father asked. "Hasn't she come home this morning?"

"No." Mrs. Pulaski shook her head, a small, rapid motion that tried to clear away unpleasant possibilities. "She's always waiting at the door when I get up in the morning. Always. I can't remember a single time when she wasn't there. But this morning she's nowhere around."

"She's probably off in the corn field, chasing mice," Mr. Pulaski offered.

That's what you think, Steve said to himself.

"Maybe she is," his mother said, but she didn't sound convinced.

"That was a good breakfast, dear." Steve's father folded his napkin and laid it at a precise right angle next to his empty bowl. He said that every morning, though every morning except Sunday he ate the same thing, two shredded-wheat biscuits with brown sugar and hot milk. And then he added, standing up, "Don't worry. I'm sure she'll be back soon. An old cat like Ginger is too wise to let anything happen." He bent over and kissed his wife on the top of the head, which was something he didn't do every morning.

Wise about everything except Celestino, Steve thought.

"Isn't that son of yours getting up this morning?" Steve's father kept his voice carefully neutral, but his mouth curved down sharply at the corners. These days "that son of yours" always referred to Matthew.

Mrs. Pulaski merely smiled her conciliatory smile. "I was going to call him as soon as I finished my coffee. I have some chores for him to do."

Mr. Pulaski grunted. "Be sure you do," he said mildly enough. "He's turning into a regular idler."

Steve picked up his bowl and began to drink the remaining milk, holding the spoon along the side of the bowl with the crook of one thumb. His favorite part of eating breakfast cereal was the undissolved sugar in the bottom of the bowl after he finished the milk. His final bite would be a spoonful of the wet, gritty sugar.

"And what are you doing today, Steve?" his father asked, surprising him into releasing the spoon so that it banged into his front teeth.

"I don't know." He set the bowl down carefully. When his father was watching him, he was very apt to spill or do something else dumb. And then, getting an inspiration, he offered, "Look for Ginger, maybe."

His father frowned. "I'm sure Ginger will come home on her own. It isn't as if she's been sick or anything like that."

"But still," Steve replied earnestly, "I'd be glad to look."

"There must be other help your mother needs. With Matthew" – his father hesitated, brushed something invisible off the front of his shirt – "the way he's been, she needs to be able to count on you."

"I cut the grass the day before yesterday," Steve said, studying the remaining milk in his bowl. The sugar would all be dissolved before he could get to it. "And raked it, too." He eyed the sugar bowl, wondering if anyone would comment on his weight, or his teeth, if he put in another spoonful and drank the milk while the sugar was still a sweet, soggy pile in the bottom of the bowl.

"Yes, I know," his father replied, his voice going gruff the way it always did when he was about to deliver a compliment. "And you did a good job, too. But," he added, "as you said, that was two days ago. I'm sure there's something your mother needs done today."

"Steve will help if I need it." His mother stood up and kissed his father on the cheek. "Right now I guess what I would like more than anything is to have him look for Ginger. I know it's silly, but I'm a little worried."

"Sure, Mom." Steve scooted from his chair, leaving the last of the milk. "I'll start right now."

His father, who wouldn't argue if that was what his wife wanted, nodded, closed the screen door quietly behind himself, and started off across the backyard, heading for the mill.

Steve waited until he had turned the corner behind the chicken coop before banging out the door behind him.

Once outside, he stopped, balancing on the back steps. Where did he think he was going, anyway? He knew where Ginger was, or if not where she was, he knew who had her and what he had to do to get her back. To get Ginger back and the letter.

He had to steal dynamite from the quarry.

He might be a liar, but he had never stolen anything in his life. Taking Donny's bike for a little while didn't really count as stealing. It only counted as dumb. But if he got caught even going into the quarry – let alone messing around with the dynamite – it was hard to imagine what the consequences would be. His father might even get into trouble with Mr. Hansen.

Unless he could get Becca to go with him. The superintendent of the whole mill could hardly fire himself for something his daughter did. Could he?

Becca was mad at him, though. Why would she help?

Still, she hadn't been along when they brought the letter. She might be mad at the other kids, too. She might be more mad at them than she was at Steve. So it was worth a try.

"I'm going, Mom," he called back. "I'm going looking."

It wasn't a lie, he told himself as he started toward the field. He *was* going looking. He was looking for dynamite.

Becca was on her front sidewalk playing hopscotch when Steve got there. She threw her marker onto the chalked hopscotch, a chain bracelet that made a metallic, slithering sound scooting across the concrete toward the number eight.

"You missed," Steve said, coming up behind her.

"No, I didn't. It's in the eight. See?"

"But part of it's in the seven. You can't have it sprawling over the line that way."

"Since when do boys make up the rules for hopscotch?" she asked, tossing her ponytail and jumping, landing with a foot on the one and the other foot on the two.

Steve sat down in the grass beside the sidewalk and waited for her to be done. When she had hopped back, holding the chain, she asked, "What are you doing here?"

The question seemed neutral. Steve couldn't tell if she was still angry with him or not.

"Did you know about the letter?" he asked.

"Did they really write it? I told them it was the dumbest idea I ever heard."

"They really wrote it," Steve replied glumly. "They came and read it to me. They wanted me to sign it, too."

"Did you?" Becca stood with her fists cocked on her hips.

"What do you take me for?"

Becca shrugged. "I don't know. Not any friend of Matthew's, that's for sure."

Steve stared at Becca for a moment, then looked away. She was right. He wasn't any friend of Matthew's, and Matthew hadn't done a thing to hurt him. He had been sad about the killing . . . that was all. Steve had been sad about the killing, too. And that was why he'd pretended all through the war that Matthew wasn't shooting at real people.

Steve didn't understand the adult world. He didn't understand it at all. They brought you up teaching you it was wrong to hurt people, and then they put you in the army and sent you out to kill.

"Anyway," he said. "I'm sorry . . . now."

Becca snorted to show what she thought of "sorry."

"You might as well know," Steve added, "it's worse than that. Celestino doesn't just have the letter; he has Ginger, too."

"How did that happen?" Becca demanded, and Steve explained.

When he was through, Becca plopped down in the grass where she sat cross-legged, her face indecipherable. "What are we going to do?"

Steve shrugged. Did she think he would be sitting there if he knew what to do?

Becca propped her chin in her hands, scowling with concentration. He waited. She was sure to think of something.

After a long silence, Becca straightened up slowly, dropping her hands to her lap. "There's no other way," she said solemnly. "We'll have to get some dynamite for Celestino."

Steve yanked at a handful of grass. It came up by the roots. "That's what I've been figuring," he said, "but it's got me worried. What if Celestino hurts somebody with the stuff?"

Becca smiled. "That's the beauty of it. He can't."

"Oh, come on now. Sure he can."

Becca shook her head, and her ponytail flapped back and forth.

Steve was impatient. "This is dynamite we're talking about, not Fourth of July firecrackers."

Becca shrugged. "So? Big deal. Dynamite's not good for much."

Steve slapped his forehead, rolled his eyes. He had never seen Becca so dumb.

"Unless," Becca added, drawing the word out until it hissed, "you mean to bring him blasting caps, too." Her eyes were sparkling.

"What are blasting caps?" It was obvious there was a catch in this discussion.

"They're the things that make the dynamite go off. You can't do a thing with dynamite without a blasting cap. It won't even burn."

Steve was skeptical. "Are you sure?"

Becca was sure, but then Becca was always sure.

"How do you know about dynamite?"

"My father told me. He even took me to the quarry once to see some blasting. He's always explaining things to me." She wrinkled her nose. "Sometimes it drives me crazy."

"You mean we could bring Celestino some dynamite, and he couldn't do anything with it?" Steve couldn't quite get the idea through his head.

"Dynamite doesn't even have a fuse," Becca explained, always willing to be the teacher. "It's the blasting cap has the fuse."

At first Steve was excited. How much fun it would be to deliver real dynamite to Celestino, to get Ginger back – and the letter, of course – and then to see him try to use it and not be able to get the littlest bang. But then he remembered, and his excitement faded. "But that would be stealing," he said, "and from the mill."

"I know," Becca said. "I think it'll be kind of fun. I've never stolen anything before . . . not for real, I mean."

"Rebecca Hansen." Steve shook his head gravely. "You've got the most criminal mind I've ever encountered!"

Becca smiled modestly.

CHAPTER 14

Steve and Becca met along the tracks that ran through the mill shortly after the four o'clock whistle had blown for the change of shift. The two night shifts were much lighter than the day shift, and no one worked in the quarry after four.

They walked single file along the tracks, Becca balancing on one rail, Steve stepping from tie to tie. *It's all right,* Steve kept saying to himself. *It's for a good cause, getting Ginger back and keeping Matthew out of prison.*

Soon they left the tracks and followed the path through the woods. The quarry was on the other side of a river. The men driving heavy equipment there had to go around by the highway, but the rest just walked from the mill, through the woods, and across a swinging bridge.

The swinging bridge was a bridge slung on steel cable from the bluff on one side of the river to the bluff that formed the edge of the quarry on the other. It was only wide enough for one person to walk at a time, and it swayed and jiggled with every step. It was strong, perfectly safe – Steve's father had told him that – but he had hated it ever since a time when he was several years younger.

Some big boys had caught him in the middle of the bridge and had thought it terribly funny to stand at each end and jump. This sent snaking humps through the entire floor, making Steve drop to his stomach and hang on for dear life. There was nothing else he could do. After the boys left, he had crawled the length of the bridge to get off. He couldn't make himself stand up and walk. Steve hadn't been near the bridge since that day. Another reason not to go stealing dynamite from the quarry.

"Ah . . . Becca?" Steve said when they arrived at the bridge.

Becca had run out ahead several feet onto the bridge and was bending her knees, bouncing up and down. She held the cables that formed hand rails and made the entire bridge react like a whip. She looked back questioningly.

"Why don't you go on across. I'll come in just a minute."

Becca gave one last mighty bounce and turned around, riding with the swells that passed beneath her feet. "Why?"

Because I have to go pee, Steve was going to say, but then he remembered his promise to himself. No more lies. "Because I've always been kind of scared of that thing. I don't like anybody making it move when I'm on it."

"Oh. Sure." Becca accepted that easily, and she turned back and skipped across to the other side and then stood waiting for Steve to follow.

See, Steve said to himself as he stepped warily onto the bridge, *it's easier to tell the truth than it is to lie.*

"It's some hole, isn't it?" Steve said as they stood on the rim of the quarry looking down into the huge cavity in the ground, probably a half-mile in diameter at its widest point.

There were several large buildings to house or repair equipment, a system of gigantic buckets that carried the crushed limestone from the quarry to the mill, and scooping and crushing machinery sitting, like sleeping beasts, on the floor of the quarry. From this distance everything – the buckets, now still for the night, and the huge Caterpillars and steam shovels – looked child-sized, miniature. But Steve knew they were actually so large he could have walked through the scoop of the steam shovel without ever ducking his head. The shovels were diesel-powered, though people still called them steam shovels.

"This way," Becca said, and Steve followed around the curving road that led to the bottom of the quarry.

"Are you sure nobody's here?" he asked, peering around uneasily when they got to the quarry floor. The huge cavity lay deep in purple shadows, and everything had taken on an eerie, fluuorescent radiance.

Becca shrugged. "We'll look around before we touch anything. If anybody turns up, we'll just say we're playing. The worst they can do is to chase us out."

And tell my father they saw me here, Steve thought.

But they found no one. The two of them checked out each of the buildings carefully, the watchman's shack last. In the shack, there was a calendar with an almost naked lady on it that made Steve's face go hot, but Becca just stared at it curiously and then turned away.

"The dynamite's stored over here," she said, hurrying toward a large metal box, big enough to walk into.

Steve followed, glancing once over his shoulder in the direction of the picture. The lady was wearing high-heeled shoes and silk stockings and . . . well, not much of anything else. She was named Miss August, and Steve couldn't help wondering what the other months were like.

The large metal box that Becca said the dynamite was stored in was locked.

"What do they lock it for if dynamite's no good without a blasting cap?" Steve asked.

"Just to be safe, I guess."

"Well, it's safe from us. That's for sure." Steve gave the padlock a tug, but it was firm.

There was another large metal box just like the first one a couple of hundred feet away. They tried that one. It was locked as well.

"Why are there two . . . and so far apart?" Steve asked.

Becca scratched her head. "I think one has the dynamite and the other one has the caps. They keep them far apart so if lightning hit the caps, it couldn't make the dynamite blow up, too."

Steve nodded. That made sense. "Well, what are we going to do now?"

"I guess there's nothing to do but go back," Becca said. "You can see it's all locked up."

Steve was exasperated. "But you must have known it would be locked before we came. What did we come here for then?"

"I thought somebody might have forgotten. I thought we might find one open or something."

Steve batted at the padlock. "So now we've got no way to get Ginger back . . . or the letter."

"If you'd – " Becca started to say, but Steve interrupted her.

"I know. If I'd kept my big mouth shut, Matthew and

Ginger wouldn't be in this mess. Do you think I don't know that?" He turned and headed back toward the watchman's cabin. "I'm going to see if I can find a file or something to open that lock."

He stepped inside the door. The calendar was still there . . . of course. He wondered what Miss September would be wearing, or not wearing. He approached the wall, ready to turn the page, when he thought of Becca, how she would tease him if she came back and found him checking out the pictures. He looked around the small shack to see what else was there.

At first he saw nothing, just an uncomfortable-looking wooden chair with one leg shorter than the others, a workbench along one wall, a stack of old newspapers. It must be a dreary place to work in practically every night. The windows were so layered with dust that Mr. Celestino would hardly be able to look out to see anything he was supposed to be watching.

Steve was about to step out and go to check the big building where the equipment was repaired when he noticed something on the floor in one corner beneath the workbench. It was a box about three times the size of a brick. He picked it up and blew the dust off the cover. DANGEROUS EXPLOSIVES, it said in bright orange letters. And then in a bold black band, diagonally across the box, it said, KEEP FROM CHILDREN.

"Becca," he called, "I think I've found some dynamite."

When she got there, Becca took the box from him and opened the lid slowly and carefully.

"What are those?" Steve asked, leaning over the open box. It was half-filled with small metal tubes, about the size of pencils but with strings – Steve supposed they were fuses – coming out of one end. "That's not dynamite."

"No, it's not," Becca said, picking one up and rolling it between her fingers. "This is a blasting cap."

Steve peered at the thing, took it between his own finger and thumb. "It doesn't look dangerous," he protested. "It doesn't look like anything at all."

Becca shrugged. "I suppose it's not unless somebody lights it."

"I have an idea," he said. "Why don't we take a blasting cap to Celestino? I can tell him I couldn't get the dynamite so I brought him a blasting cap instead. It'll be better than nothing. He might even get a bang out of it."

"Ha, ha," Becca said, unamused. "Very funny. But what if the cap hurts somebody? It says KEEP FROM CHILDREN on the lid."

Steve scoffed, "Adults would label the whole world KEEP FROM CHILDREN if they could – everything but school. That doesn't mean a thing. It wouldn't have to be very strong to set the dynamite off."

Becca wasn't convinced; Steve could tell that. But before she could protest further, a voice came from the other side of the quarry. "Hey, you! What are you doing in there?"

Someone must have seen them enter the shack! Steve's breath caught in his chest and wouldn't start up again. All the color had drained from Becca's face. They stood there, rooted to the floor of the shack.

"Run," Becca gasped finally. "We've got to get out of here!" She set the box down on the workbench and turned on her heel and ran. Steve hesitated, alone in the shack, then slid the long, shiny blasting cap he had been holding into his back pocket and followed as fast as his legs would carry him.

They ran up the winding road out of the quarry until the man who had been approaching from the other side, waving, looked like a toy.

"And stay out of this quarry!" the man called after them.

Steve followed immediately behind Becca, even across the bridge. When they got to the other side, they ran a short distance into the woods and collapsed, gasping. Steve had a stitch in his side that he figured would probably ache like that for the rest of his life.

It was only after they were beginning to breathe normally again that Steve turned around and showed Becca the slender, silver tube extending above his back pocket.

"I don't think you should have done that," she said, shaking her head.

"Where have you been?" Steve's father asked sternly. "You're late for supper again."

"In the quarry, sir," Steve replied. He might as well tell the truth. The man who had chased them out probably recognized them anyway.

"What were you doing in the quarry?" Matthew interjected, his question sounding merely curious, not cross like their father's.

"Looking for Ginger," Steve replied. Maybe another time he would tell the whole truth. There were times when a small lie was only prudent.

"Looking for Ginger? In the quarry!" Steve couldn't tell if his father was more enraged or simply astonished. "What on earth made you think Ginger might have been in the quarry?"

"Well," Steve explained, "it was the one place I could think of where she might have gotten hurt so she couldn't make it home. I thought she could be there, buried under some rocks. I thought she might need help." His mother's face took on a rumpled look, and Steve wished he hadn't been quite so graphic.

"You thought. You thought!" his father repeated. "The trouble is, you didn't think at all. You're the one who might have been hurt. You know you're not allowed in that quarry, not anywhere near it. There's blasting. There's big machinery. There're possible cave-ins. There is every harm you can imagine waiting for a boy in that place – and some you can't imagine."

"Yes, sir." Steve felt the slender blasting cap that he had stuck in the waist of his jeans, hidden under his shirt at the side.

"You say 'yes, sir,'" his father said, "but I wish I could be sure you were really hearing me."

"Oh, I'm hearing. I am." Steve nodded his head vigorously to show how well he was hearing. He had to hold his arm tight against his side to keep the cap in place, and the sweat was starting to trickle down, making the metal rod slippery. He was afraid the cap was going to slip right through and come out the bottom of his pant leg. He wondered if a blasting cap could go off from being dropped onto a linoleum floor. He wondered how big a noise a blasting cap made. If it went off, he wouldn't be able to make up any story to explain it away; he was sure of that.

"I'm sorry, Steve," his father was running his fingers through his hair in the same way Matthew did, "but I think you're going to have to go up to bed without any supper. Maybe that will help you to remember next time."

Steve screwed his face into a look of appropriate disappointment as he squeezed his arm tighter over the cap. The look of disappointment wasn't too hard to accomplish, even though he wanted desperately to be dismissed from the kitchen while he still had a hold on the hidden cap. Supper was fried chicken, mashed potatoes and corn on the cob.

"You can go now," his father said wearily, and Steve made his escape. His legs would barely support him for the climb up the stairs, but unfortunately his brain wasn't tired enough to leave him alone. DANGER, a warning voice kept repeating somewhere in the back of his skull. EXPLOSIVES. KEEP FROM CHILDREN.

CHAPTER 15

The next morning Steve telephoned Becca, and they met in the middle of the alfalfa field. Steve held open the grocery sack he was carrying for Becca to peer into.

"What's that?" she asked. "Where did you get it?"

"What does it look like?" Steve pulled a cluster of dull red tubes from the sack and held them up. A fuse extended from the one in the center of the bunch.

Becca made a full circle around Steve, examining the tubes he held from every angle. "Well, I would say it looks like dynamite, but dynamite's not red, at least not the stuff my dad showed me."

"Oh." Steve was disappointed. "Well . . . Celestino won't know that."

"No. I suppose he won't. But what is it . . . really?"

Steve grinned. "Old railroad flares, burned-out ones I picked up along the tracks . . . from my collection."

Becca grinned back. "Wonderful! How'd you ever think of it?"

"Well," Steve said, modestly enough, "I got to looking at the blasting cap, and I was afraid Celestino wouldn't trade anything for that. It doesn't look like much. So I fixed up something that would look better. I tried painting paper-towel tubes red first, but that didn't work. They just looked like red paper-towel tubes."

"Didn't your mother or Matthew or somebody see you with the paint? Didn't you have to explain?"

Steve shrugged. "Mostly all I had to explain was why I was using my toothbrush to paint with. When my mother saw me, she got so upset about me ruining it that she never asked why I wanted red paper-towel rollers."

Becca nodded her approval. "These are perfect. I mean, they look real."

"You said dynamite isn't red, though."

"What I saw was kind of yellow-brown, but if Celestino doesn't know about blasting caps, he won't know the difference. Dynamite is always red in the funny papers."

"Speaking of blasting caps . . ." Steve tugged on the fuse in the center flare, and the slim metal cap emerged.

Becca gasped. "You mean you're going to give Celestino that?"

"I filled all the flares with wet sand and put in the blasting cap to make it seem real. I figure that way he'll get enough of a bang so maybe he'll think I really gave him dynamite."

Becca had pulled the end of her ponytail around and was chewing on it. The hair made a grinding sound between her teeth that brought out goose bumps on Steve's arms. "I don't know about that cap," she said. "I don't think you should give it to him. They do explode, you know."

"But that's the point. If nothing happens, Celestino will see I gave him fakes. Then he'll come back and get me, or maybe Ginger. But if it blows up . . . just a little . . . he'll think he did something wrong himself."

"I suppose you're right," Becca said, but she didn't sound very certain.

"I figure when he lights it, he'll get a little bang and a lot of wet sand." Steve dropped the flares back into the bag. "Anyway, let's go find Celestino. I can't wait to see my mother's face when I bring Ginger back. She's sure something's happened to her by now."

"She'll really be glad to see that old cat, won't she?" Becca said as she fell into step beside Steve.

"Me, too," Steve replied, adding to himself, *And I'll be glad to quit worrying about Matthew getting arrested.*

When they arrived at Celestino's house, they found him sitting on his front porch steps between the twins.

"You mean you really got it?" Celestino stood up and reached for the bundle of flares Steve had held up while he was still coming up the walk. Steve stepped back, hugging them against his chest.

"Wait up," he said. "First we get Ginger – and the letter – then you can have your dynamite." He didn't want Celestino examining the flares too closely too soon.

Celestino's eyes narrowed suspiciously. "How do I know that ain't some kind of fake if you won't let me look at it?"

"Here, I'll prove it's real," Becca said, and she pulled the blasting cap out from the center stick.

Celestino squinted at the blasting cap dubiously. "What's that?" he asked.

"Don't you know?" Becca was putting on her superior tone. "It's a blasting cap. If Steve hadn't brought you one of these, the dynamite wouldn't do you a bit of good. You wouldn't have been able to set it off."

"She's right," Kenny said, coming down the steps to stand by Celestino. "You have to have a blasting cap to make dynamite go."

Celestino looked down at Kenny, frowning. "Why didn't you tell me before?"

Kenny shrugged. "I wasn't around when you made your deal, or I would have. When you told me about it, I didn't think about a blasting cap."

Celestino peered at the cap extending from the center of the bundle of flares. Steve eased it out a few more inches so he could see it better. "See?" he said. "You're all set up." Then he tucked the cap in again and dropped the flares back into the grocery bag. "I want the letter first," he said. "Then Ginger."

A sly look slipped across Celestino's face. "What if I've already mailed the letter?"

"Then," Steve said, keeping his voice steady and cool with great effort, "I give you the dynamite you bargained for to return Ginger, but I keep the blasting cap." He slipped the silver tube out of the bundle of flares and held it in his hand. "You only asked for dynamite," he reminded Celestino.

Celestino's face was getting red. For a moment he stood there, glaring down at Steve, and Steve had the scary feeling that Celestino was going to take the whole thing by force and not keep any part of his bargain. But then the older boy shrugged and reached for his back pocket. "Okay, Pulaski. You win this time," he said.

Steve smiled and returned the blasting cap to its place in the middle of the flares.

"Here's the letter." Celestino pulled a creased envelope out of his back pocket and handed it to Steve. The envelope was addressed to J. Edgar Huver, FBI, Wash. D.C. It had a three-cent stamp on it, ready to go. Steve tore the envelope and its contents in half, then into quarters and stuffed the scraps into his own back pocket.

"Now I want Ginger," he said. "Then you can have the dynamite, blasting cap and all."

"All right," Celestino conceded. "This way." He started down the street in the direction of the cluster of garages. Kenny and Becca fell in behind him. Donny followed, walking next to Steve.

When they arrived at the row of garages, Celestino pulled open the swinging door to his family's garage.

I should have thought of looking here, Steve thought. *Could have saved Becca and myself a whole lot of trouble.* But even after they had walked into the shadowy darkness of the garage, Ginger was nowhere to be seen.

"Where've you got her?" Steve demanded. And then he called, "Ginger! Here, kitty-kitty-kitty."

The garage was dark and silent.

"Hold your horses," Celestino grumbled, and he reached into his pocket and brought out a key, which he inserted into the trunk of the black 1936 Ford that occupied most of the space in the garage. The rest formed a silent U around Celestino, waiting for Ginger to emerge.

"Come on, cat," Celestino said, not unkindly, as the lid swung open. "You can go home now," and he bent over the dark cavern of the trunk. But then he remained bent over there, his body frozen into position.

"What's the matter?" Steve asked, stepping forward, trying to see beyond Celestino into the trunk of the car. "Isn't she there?"

"Of course she's here," Celestino snapped. "Do you think she could get out? She's just . . . sleeping."

"Well, wake her up, then." Steve moved in closer to the car, trying to jostle Celestino aside. To his surprise, Celestino gave ground, and Steve found himself alone, peering into the shadowy compartment.

Ginger lay there, stretched out on her side, her golden eyes that caught the dusty light filtering in from the door wide open, the mouth open, too, a pink, flannel tongue protruding beyond the tiny points of her teeth. Steve reached his free hand out cautiously and touched her striped fur. It felt as it always did, soft and luxuriant, but the body beneath the fur was stiff.

Steve turned on Celestino. "Liar!" he exploded. "Don't tell me she's sleeping! You can see for yourself. Ginger's dead!"

Celestino backed off, raising one arm to cover his face as if he were warding off a blow, and his voice was shrill. "I never hurt her!" he cried. "I never did. I don't know what happened, but I never hurt her at all!" And then he turned and ran, leaving Steve and Becca and the twins staring after him.

Steve looked back inside the car trunk, wishing this were

all a dream, wishing he would find it empty this time. But there she lay, his mother's pet who had been part of the family for longer than he had, her chin lifted, revealing the gleaming patch of white where she had always liked to be scratched.

"I don't think he meant – " Kenny started to say.

"It doesn't matter what Celestino meant," Donny interrupted. "Ginger's dead."

They formed a procession down the street, Steve in the lead with the rigid form that had once been Ginger cradled in his arms, Becca following immediately behind, carrying the bag of "dynamite," and then the twins, jostling each other off the sidewalk to keep right after Becca.

Ginger was dead. It seemed impossible, looking at her, feeling her soft fur, to believe that she wasn't going to begin breathing any minute, begin purring and bumping her hard little head against Steve, demanding attention. She was dead, and that was final, as final as anything could ever be.

Steve hadn't cried. None of them had. But Steve supposed the others, from their silence, had been feeling the same thing as he – a queer kind of emptiness that seemed to reach down inside of him to his very toes. He didn't know what he was going to say to his mother, how he could possibly explain. He could blame it on Celestino, of course, but somehow that wouldn't help. Besides, his mother would never believe Celestino would do such a thing just out of meanness. She would want to know how he had been provoked. His mother never believed that anyone was mean for no reason, even though people sometimes were.

They found Steve's mother in the garden, picking beans.

She was kneeling between the rows, one hand holding up the leafy plants, the other plucking the long, curving green beans and dropping them into a basket at her side. She looked up as Steve approached, and her welcoming smile froze when her eyes came to rest on the still, stiff form suspended between Steve's extended arms.

"Oh," she said. "Oh!" And she put one hand to her throat as if someone had hurt her there. She got to her feet awkwardly and reached out to take Ginger into her own arms.

"What happened?" she asked, her eyes pooling with tears. "Where did you find her?" She held Ginger against her breasts as if that would make the cat warm again, pliable and alive.

"She was shut in the Celestinos' garage," Steve answered, truthfully. At least it was a piece of the truth.

Mrs. Pulaski ran her hand the length of Ginger's body, checking her for injury. "It must have been so hot in there," she murmured, "and no water. She would have been upset, too. Terribly upset." She hugged Ginger tightly. "She's such an old cat. I suppose she could have had a heart attack . . . or maybe a stroke." She looked at Steve as if for confirmation.

Steve nodded, his mouth dry, his throat burning. "I suppose she could have," he said. The others stood in a small semicircle behind him, clearing their throats quietly from time to time, but otherwise saying nothing.

"Steve," his mother said, and she thrust Ginger toward him as if she had only that moment realized the cat she held was dead, "would you bury her for me, please? I . . . I don't believe I could."

Steve took the rigid, furry body back into his arms, nodding wordlessly. His mother picked up her basket of beans, though she had harvested only half the length of the row, and walked toward the house, holding herself stiffly erect. When she got to the back steps, her head bowed and her shoulders hunched forward and she ran up the steps, letting the screen door slam shut behind her.

The group stood in silence, continuing to watch the door.

"Why didn't you tell her?" Kenny asked.

Steve shrugged. "There was too much to tell," he said. "I wouldn't have known where to begin." *Or what to leave out,* he thought.

"Let's have a funeral," Becca suggested. "I'll be the preacher."

CHAPTER 16

"Receive this cat in heaven," Becca commanded God in what Steve hoped was her concluding prayer. "She was a good cat. She never scratched anybody, and she never bit, and if she killed mice sometimes – and baby rabbits – that was only because You made her that way."

Steve looked down at the white-wrapped bundle in the bottom of the hole they had dug behind the chicken coop. They hadn't been able to find a box the right size, so Steve had gotten a torn sheet from the rag drawer in the kitchen. His mother had been sitting at the kitchen table, not doing a thing, her eyes all red and the tip of her nose red, too, when Steve had gone in for the piece of old sheet.

"Thank you, sweetie," she had said in a small voice when he started out again with the material in his hand. He had nodded and slipped quietly out the door, his cheeks burning with shame. She wouldn't thank him if she knew the whole story.

"And now for the eulogy," Becca was saying.

"What's that?" Kenny asked, obviously impatient. He was holding a shovel full of dirt, ready to begin filling in the grave.

"That's when the preacher talks about what a good person – cat – Ginger was and how we all loved her and how much we're going to miss her but how she's happier in heaven."

Steve wondered if cats had their own heaven. What would cat heaven be like? An endless corn field filled with mice? That wouldn't be heaven for the mice, though, would it? If there was such a thing as a heaven for cats, there wouldn't be any bullies like Celestino to shut them up in the trunks of cars, that was for sure.

"Well, get on with it," Kenny growled, and Becca began on the eulogy.

Steve didn't listen. Instead he relived his late-night encounter with Celestino . . . the menacing way Celestino had run his hand over Ginger's head, pushing her ears back, squeezing her; the way she had purred in Celestino's arms, not even sensing her own danger.

It was all Celestino's fault, the whole thing. Celestino should have known better than to shut an old cat up in a car trunk for nearly two days. He should have known better than to write that letter to the FBI, too.

Becca was finally running out of words. "God bless this cat," she concluded at last, "and keep her from harm. Amen."

As if any further harm could come to her, Steve thought, and he turned away as Kenny dropped the first shovelful of dirt onto the wrapped form.

By the time the twins had tamped the dirt down, Steve was ready to face them again. "I've been thinking," he said. "Will anybody here help me get Celestino . . . pay him back?"

Kenny and Donny looked at each other, passing some wordless message the way they frequently did, and then they looked back at Steve. "Sure," they said together.

But then Donny asked, "What are we going to do?"

"We're going to capture him," Steve explained, "and tie him up and set off the dynamite he wanted, right in front of him."

The twins blanched and stepped back. Even Becca looked doubtful, but when Steve was through explaining that the dynamite was merely sand-packed railroad flares with one blasting cap, Kenny and Donny thought it a wonderful idea.

"I don't know, Steve," Becca said, shaking her head. "I'm not sure how strong those blasting caps are."

"Don't be a sissy," Kenny said. "It's not real dynamite Steve's got."

Becca protested instantly. "I'm not a sissy!"

"Then help us get Celestino," Kenny challenged.

For a minute Becca hesitated, her eyes skipping from one boy's face to the other, but then she thrust her chin out and said, "Okay. I'll help."

"How will we get him tied up?" Donny asked. "He's pretty strong."

Steve spoke up again. "I've got it all figured out. You and Kenny go find him and pretend you want to play, out at the foxhole. Pretend you don't care anything about him killing Ginger."

"Then, when we get him out there," Donny filled in, "you and Becca can jump him, just the way we did to you."

"Right," Steve said. "That's exactly right."

"Here they come," Becca whispered. "Be ready." She was fingering a length of the rope they had found in the weeds. It was part of the rope that had been used on them.

Steve and Becca were crouching behind a dense bush at the edge of the clearing. Steve could hear movement coming toward the other side of the clearing and the twins talking steadily. He couldn't hear anyone answering, but he assumed it was Celestino they were talking to.

"We've got to get around farther," Steve whispered. "We'll have to come from behind if we're going to take him by surprise."

Becca nodded, and they crouched down, taking cover first behind the wide trunk of an old tree, then behind another bush, as they moved toward the other side of the clearing.

They got there just in time to see the twins, with Celestino between them, emerge into the long grass.

"Now!" Steve said in a low voice, and he and Becca sprang, simultaneously, toward the tall figure.

When the twins heard them coming, they grabbed Celestino's arms, holding him tightly. At first Celestino seemed so taken by surprise that he was rigid, making no attempt to shake the twins off, but as soon as Becca's rope looped around his head and then dropped to his chest, he began struggling with real fervor.

Steve was having a hard time getting a good hold any place, because Celestino was fighting so fiercely and there were so many hands on him. Steve grabbed the back of Celestino's collar and hung on, planting his feet. It was one of the things he was good at, keeping his ground in games like tug-of-war. But to his surprise the shirt began to tear, splitting quickly from top to bottom, laying Celestino's back bare.

When Steve first saw Celestino's skin he gasped, let go, and stood staring. Celestino's entire back was crisscrossed with faint red lines.

So that was the noise Steve had heard when he was waiting outside Celestino's house for his drunken father to go to work. Celestino's father beat him. And that was why Celestino never went without a shirt like the other boys did, because he was hiding the evidence.

"Come on, Steve. Help us!" Kenny panted, and Steve joined the fray again, but much of his enthusiasm for the fight had mysteriously ebbed away.

Finally they had Celestino tied securely against the old oak tree on the edge of the clearing. No one but Steve seemed to have noticed the secret of Celestino's back, and for some reason Steve couldn't have explained, he was glad the others hadn't seen.

Celestino was panting, bruised, but the rest of them were hot and disheveled and bruised as well.

"Now you've got me," Celestino sneered, "whatcha gonna do with me?"

"We have plans," Steve said quietly, and then he turned to Becca and commanded, "Go get the dynamite."

Becca nodded obediently and went.

She came back with the bundle of flares, the fused blasting cap protruding from the middle. Holding the flares at arm's length as if they might blow up without provocation, she asked, "Where should we set it up?"

For a moment Steve almost relented, almost decided not to go through with the ruse. Then he remembered the sound of the dry dirt dropping into Ginger's grave, and he said, "Two feet away will be far enough. We don't want the body in too many pieces."

Celestino blanched, but he didn't say a word.

Kenny and Donny pulled away the grass and found a stout stick to scoop out a small hole so the flares would stand upright.

"Anybody got a match?" Kenny asked.

"Just a minute," Celestino said finally, his voice cracking. "You guys can't be serious."

Donny looked him straight in the eye. "We're as serious as you were when you killed Ginger," he said.

"But that was an accident! I was just hiding her there. I didn't mean for her to die." Sweat was beginning to pop out on his forehead.

"Sure," Kenny said. "Sure."

"Come on, you guys," Celestino pleaded.

Steve wiped his hands on his jeans, wondering why he wasn't enjoying this whole thing more. Celestino was his enemy, wasn't he?

"Here," Becca said. "I have matches." She brought out a book of paper matches and held them toward Steve.

"You can light it," Steve said, taking a step back and nodding in Becca's direction.

Becca shook her head firmly. "It's your dynamite. You're the one who brought it back from the quarry."

"And Ginger was your mom's cat," Donny supplied.

"And it was your brother Celestino was gonna turn in to the FBI," Kenny added.

You'd think Celestino wrote that letter all by himself, Steve thought. He took the matches from Becca's hand.

"Hey," Celestino said. "Hey!" But he didn't seem able to say anything more.

Steve knelt in front of the "dynamite," and though he knew it was a fake – of course it was fake; he was the one who had put it together, wasn't he? – his hand trembled as he tore out a match. He closed the matchbook carefully, as his father had taught him to do. He almost giggled to himself as he did so. Were safety rules important when you were about to execute somebody?

"You can't – " Celestino's breath was coming in gurgling gasps. "I mean, you're gonna go to prison for this. You'll get the electric chair." He was struggling against the ropes, but it was no use. They had tied him well.

Steve struck the match, but it bent and fizzled. He dropped that match in the grass and took out another, again carefully closing the paper matchbook. He struck it and got a rush of sparks and fire that settled immediately to an orange, tear-shaped flame. He moved his hand toward the fuse of the blasting cap. He could hear Celestino draw in his breath.

"Come on, Steve," Becca said, "before you burn your fingers."

"Yeah. Come on," the twins said in unison.

Again Steve had the urge to giggle. The whole thing was so ludicrous. It was important, of course, not to burn your fingers when you were about to blow somebody up. He touched the flame to the fuse, shook the match to put it out, dropped it, and stepped back.

At first he thought the blasting cap hadn't caught. In the sunlight that bore down from the nearly noontime sun, he couldn't see the fuse burning. But then he detected the blue line of fire creeping along. It was a long fuse. Of course, in the quarry the men had to have plenty of time to get far enough away to be safe.

"Everybody better back up," Becca said officiously. "We don't want it to get anybody but Celestino."

The three of them backed up, holding their perfectly straight line, nearly to the other edge of the clearing, and Steve backed up just in front of them.

The flame licked along the fuse toward the shiny metal cap and the cluster of fake dynamite.

Celestino began to cry, silently . . . terribly.

"Aw . . . look at him," Kenny said.

Donny and Becca didn't say anything. Steve was glad. He couldn't look at Celestino's face. Celestino thought he was going to die.

It's a lie, Steve thought. *It's a worse lie than any I've ever told with words.*

The fire crept closer to the blasting cap. Celestino was gritting his teeth, holding his chin up, but the tears were running down his cheeks. He wasn't making a sound, though. Not a sound.

Steve remembered, suddenly, that when he had heard the smacking sound, the repeated sharp crack of a belt or a stick, he had never heard Celestino cry out. Not once.

I can't, he thought. *It's not fair!* He lunged forward to extinguish the advancing line of flame.

And that was the instant the blasting cap blew.

CHAPTER 17

"Steve. Steve?" Matthew's face swam into view somewhere in the air above Steve's own. His face seemed to be enlarging and growing small again, as if it were a balloon someone was playing with. Steve wanted to tell whoever it was to leave Matthew alone, to leave his face alone, but it was too much effort to speak.

Celestino. Where was Celestino? Had they killed him?

Celestino had been brave. He had cried, but crying didn't mean he wasn't brave.

But the dynamite was fake. Wasn't it?

Still, something had happened.

Maybe someone had dropped an atomic bomb.

The balloon of Matthew's face had a worried frown, but it kept drifting farther away. Steve wanted to call it back, but he couldn't. He was falling in the other direction.

Falling.

Steve woke up to a vision of snow . . . everywhere. Blinding, white snow. He could see Matthew sitting in a chair in the midst of all the snow. Wasn't he cold? He was sleeping, his head dropped forward, his chin resting on his chest.

"Matthew?"

Matthew's head jerked up. "You're awake, Steve. How do you feel?"

Steve tried to feel, to know how he was, but he couldn't feel anything except pain – in his face, his chest, his arms. "I don't know," he said. "Not too good, I don't think. How am I supposed to feel?"

Matthew laughed softly. "Not too good, I don't think, but you'll get better."

Then Matthew didn't say any more and Steve allowed himself to drift for a moment in the whiteness. It wasn't snow. It was a strange room . . . everything white, the walls, the curtains, the bed. Maybe the floor was white, too. He wondered if it was. He couldn't see that. He would sit up to look at the floor later.

He remembered now. He was in the hospital. He remembered the twins and Becca leading him and Celestino down the street, both of them howling. He remembered the pain of a thousand hot needles in his face, his chest, his arms.

"How is Celestino?" he asked.

"A little better than you," Matthew answered.

That was good. At least Steve thought that was good. "And the twins?"

"They're okay. They wanted to stay to see how you were, but the doctor treated them and sent them home. The problem was the shrapnel, you know . . . from the blasting cap. Those things are deadly, Steve. You kids are lucky nobody lost an eye."

"What about Becca?"

"She's fine. I don't think she had a scratch."

"Figures."

"What did you say?"

"Nothing."

"Mom and Dad were here for hours," Matthew explained after another silence. "I finally told them to go home and get some sleep. I'm supposed to call them when you wake up." He started to get up from the chair.

"Matthew?"

"Yes?"

"Wait a little bit, will you? Before you call Mom and Dad."

Matthew hesitated, his face creased again in that worried frown. Then he sat down. "All right, just a little bit. But why?"

"Because I need to talk to you."

Matthew nodded. "Okay," he said. "Talk, buddy."

Steve licked his lips, found them covered with some kind of bad-tasting ointment. "I wanted to tell you . . . well, I don't *want* to tell you exactly, but I need to. I've been making up lies . . . about you. One real bad one."

Matthew waited, not saying anything, and Steve took a deep breath. "I told the kids that you never killed anybody in the war, that you used to adjust the big gun so it would fire short . . . or long, just so it wouldn't hit anybody."

For an endless moment Matthew still didn't speak, and Steve waited, his body rigid, feeling the weight of the pain that held him down. Finally Matthew said, "And you consider that a real bad lie?"

"It was. Celestino and the twins wrote a letter to tell J. Edgar Hoover. They told him what you said about being ashamed and the lie I told them, about you not killing anybody in the whole war. They figured you'd go to prison for treason."

Matthew laid a big hand on top of Steve's head. "I wish your lie were true, Steve. I wish that gun hadn't been aimed at a single other human being."

Steve twisted in the bed so he could see Matthew more clearly. How familiar that square-jawed, gentle face was, every inch of it familiar except for the pain etched around the mouth. "I wish it, too," he said softly. "For the whole war I was wishing it for you."

Matthew tried to smile, but the smile didn't quite succeed.

"Anyway," Steve added, "I got the letter back. It's what I was going to trade the dynamite for, the fake dynamite and the blasting cap. I was going to trade it for the letter and Ginger."

"Only Ginger was dead, so you used the blasting cap on Celestino . . . right?"

Steve nodded, and Matthew sighed.

"Well, maybe you've learned what the world still hasn't."

"What's that?"

"That you can't hurt other people without hurting yourself."

Steve raised one hand to the bandages on his face.

"Inside, too, Steve," Matthew said.

Steve could feel it, the hurt inside. At least he thought he could feel what Matthew was talking about. He wondered what it would be like to face Celestino after this.

Pretty bad.

Or his mother, once she knew Ginger's death was partly his fault.

Or himself.

Again a silence lay between Steve and Matthew, but it was a comfortable silence, carrying no extra freight with it. Lying there, feeling the fierce burning of his skin, Steve remembered the cooling night swims Matthew had taken him for when he was small.

"Matthew," Steve asked, "did you ever take Seiji out to swim in the stars?"

Matthew looked surprised. He started to turn away, but then he didn't. He stared at Steve, shaking his head. "He wouldn't have understood. We couldn't talk to one another, you know."

"I don't think it would have mattered. I always slept better after those swims . . . even though I knew."

"That I had lied?" Matthew asked. "About the stars being made of ice?"

"They told us in science . . . a long time ago . . . long before you ever went off to the war."

"But still you slept better?" Matthew's hand touched the edge of the bed, hesitated, reached over to cover Steve's.

Steve shrugged, returned the light pressure on his hand. "Sure. I never could figure why, but I did."

Matthew bent over and blew a clump of hair off Steve's forehead. His breath was like a night breeze.

"I'm not going to tell lies anymore," Steve said. "Not ever." And then he thought a moment and added, "At least not so many."

"Maybe I should make that promise, too," Matthew said.

"No." Steve shook his head, mindful of the bandages. "Your stories were different. They made things seem better."

"What about the true stories . . . the ones that made you feel bad?"

Steve gripped his brother's hand harder. He thought of the little boy who had died while Matthew watched, of the unknown soldiers killed by Matthew's gun. He looked at his brother. His face was open and expectant, as if there were something he needed from Steve, but Steve didn't know what it could be.

Then he remembered Celestino's scarred back and the helpless terror in his eyes just before the blasting cap exploded.

"I think I understand, now," he said, "at least a little, about the things that happened in the war."

Matthew drew in a gigantic breath, as though he had been weeks without enough air. "Do you really, Steve? Do you know how I feel?"

Steve nodded. "It just gets started. You don't really know how, but it does. And there you are . . . doing things. Terrible things. And other people, too. But it's like there's no way to stop."

"And when it's all over . . ." Matthew's voice faded away.

"You don't want it to happen again. Not in a million years. So you've got to tell people what it was like . . . even if they don't want to hear."

"You really do understand," Matthew whispered.

Steve nodded, remembering Celestino, remembering what he had done to Celestino. "I guess we've both got to tell," he said. "You *and* me."

"You and *I*," Matthew corrected softly, and Steve let his painfully tight skin stretch into a smile.

"You and I," he agreed.